LOVING THE LYKOS

AMANDA KIMBERLEY

About Loving the Lykos

Life's not always a beach in the Texas heat of summer.

Colton has spent a good majority of his life steering clear of problems. But once he met his boss, trouble came knocking in the form of her high heels and bitch of a bite. He wanted nothing to do with her when he found out she turned him into a dog.

Now that he's met Harper, he wonders if he should run with his tail between his legs. Or? Should he risk telling her that her summer vacation was going to the wolves?

All Harper wanted was some fun in the sun and possibly a fling. And she only wanted to do this so she could put her ex behind her. The island resort in her home state of Texas seemed to fit the bill for both, especially on her shoestring budget.

After meeting Colton, the only problem with her plan is that she now wants the summer to last forever. Then she discovers his secret and her vacation goes south on the island. Will she want to ride out his wave? Or just swim to safer shores to lick her wounds?

CHAPTER 1

YOU MUST WEAR THE REQUIRED UNIFORM

Colton wrinkled his nose as Blake, his boss, thrust out his new and highly questionable swimsuit uniform attire in front of him. The thing would probably make him sing the high notes because two bandaids clipped together would most likely cover more of his larger-than-average junk than the Speedo she was dangling like a carrot.

Not that he had to brag about his junk—because he was comfortable with the manhood that God gave him. However, the more Colton stared at the Speedo, the more he wondered if even his balls would fit in the damned thing. It appeared he'd have not only a hard time stuffing his entire sex into it, but he'd have to go in for a wax job. There was no avoiding it. And he'd need to make sure they left him completely bare.

Just the thought had him squirming in his now suddenly constrictive pants. They felt like vice-grips as the horrors of the painful wax strips ripping off his hair and skin entered his mind. The sensation and the horrifyingly tiny Speedo made him mentally apologize to any girl he slept with that wondered if he'd fit inside of them. Then he found himself mentally apologizing to all the girls he ogled in a bikini. Clearly, karma wasn't playing fair because this was going to bite big time.

She had a smile on her face as if to symbolize that he, the dumb horse, would take her proverbial Speedo carrot as bait. To be the subject of objectification never bothered him until now. And that had a lot to do with Blake since she was his ex.

Colton was far from dumb. He had no intention of wanting to take her bait. But what else was there to do? She made him into the dog he was, and he needed the job.

Sadly, she totally had him by the balls, which clearly would now be on display for her to view anytime she wanted to at work. The sadder part was that Speedo made him feel like she was not only grabbing him but was also twisting and turning his junk just to screw with him more. The tight Speedo was just another sleazy tactic on her part to make him into the boy-toy she wanted him to be, and he was tired of it.

"What the fuck is that?"

"I told you, it's your new uniform for when you clean the pool here. As your Alpha Queen and the owner of this place, I get to decide what uniform the pool boy wears, so no lip! Besides, you'll thank me once you've experienced Texas heat in the summers. And hopefully, it's the type of thanking I'd really like from you." She said to him as she slapped his right butt cheek.

"Yeah, I highly doubt that." He said as he crossed his arms over his chest before continuing, "And I told you before, it will be a cold day in hell before I fuck the fucked up."

"Come on, Colton! How long are you going to hold that love nip against me?" She asked as she traced her index finger over a scar on his shoulder.

"A day longer than forever." He said while pulling away from her.

"You don't mean that, and you will come around. Now take the uniform. I have important events to plan so my Omegas can find mates. Next week starts Summer break for all the college students, and I want to make sure our resort is an attractive attraction to them. The pandemic killed our business, and those Omegas are horny as hell. I want them to keep their paws to themselves, so having them pursue other females will suit me just fine. The gods know I want you, and that's why I've been saving myself for you. So go on and take the uniform."

"So, you are saying that you are not only fucked up, but you are bat shit crazy, too?"

"Oh, get off it! I know for a fact that you are attracted to me."

"Past tense, bitch!"

"Watch your tongue with your Alpha Queen!" she said as she raised her hand to slap him across the cheek.

He grabbed her hand before it made contact.

"I'm only calling you the female dog that you are."

He snatched the Speedo from her other hand and spun on one heel to leave her office.

"I am royalty! A dire wolf that comes from a long line of good blood. I have given you a gift, and it's about time you understood that! You will bow to your Queen before you leave this room! Is that understood?"

Despite not wanting to do anything she said, his body reacted to her command, and he kneeled down where he stood. Damned bitch had his dog pussy-whipped the minute she bit him and turned him into a monster.

"That's better." She said while closing the distance between the two of them. She patted the top of his head before continuing, "Good boy! You'll warm up to me. I know you will. Now go put that on and clean the pool." Her smile cut through him like a blade to his gut.

"Never will I ever warm up to you."

"You are becoming quite the subservient bitch." She said as she patted the top of his head again.

"I'm only your bitch because you made me your dog."

She flashed him another steely smile.

"Dismissed."

"Yes, my Queen."

He got up from kneeling and headed to the cabana area, where he did as the bitch commanded. All the while swearing and sighing the entire time, he changed into the tight Speedo. Thankfully, his last wax job seemed to be still bikini ready, but he made a mental note to make an appointment later in the week.

His dick, however, was a completely different story. Hang right was just as uncomfortable as hanging left. Colton did his best to conceal as much as possible before stepping out to the pool area. As he reached for the pool skimmer net, he muttered a prayer to God that there were only old ladies at the loungers. Getting a hard-on was just not an option in the bandaid covering him.

He started the menial job of removing the stray hairs, bandaids, and bugs floating in the pool. He usually found more bugs than anything, including leaves. Not that there weren't trees around the resort, but mostly it was more common for the other things to surface in the water.

He let out another sigh as thoughts of the beginning of Summer entered his head. His boss had been impossible to deal with during the Spring, which was when they were dating. He couldn't imagine what Blake would be like all summer long. He knew she made him wear this thing so she could get her own rocks off, but soon the college girls would come, and he wasn't looking forward to blue balls. Because clearly, that's what he'd get in this thing if he wound up with a hard dick.

CHAPTER 2

ROGER THAT

"I don't know, guys. Maybe I should stay here for the summer and save up for that new condo development scheduled to finish by October. I've had my eye on them for a while. Since I had to move back, it's been a drag remembering how to live with my parents again. You forget how crappy it is to share a bathroom until you have to. Especially with someone that pees standing up. And not to mention the fact that my dating life will become nonexistent until I find a place of my own. There's zero privacy." Harper said to her best friends Chloe and Zoey as they all sat down for their weekly coffee get-together at the local Starbucks.

"Harper, you need this! Roger was an asshole,

and even though it was hard enough to put your tail between your legs and move back in with your mom, it would've been worse if you stayed with the ass, and you know it."

"Yeah, girl! His chauvinism was borderline abusive. You remember that." Said Chloe.

"And need we remind you of him flirting with anything on two legs—even when you were out on a date with him? The guy was a total asshat." Said Zoey.

"Chloe, Zoey, I get that you want me happy, but I'm just not sure this is a good idea right now."

"Come on! It's the trip of a lifetime. You've been moping for half the year about Roger, and it's a dirt-cheap deal. We can't pass this up!"

"Chloe, it's dirt-cheap because the pandemic made us all stay in—and? We are not leaving the freaking state," Harper said with a chuckle.

"Hey! Don't hate on the trip to Pearl South Padre! It doesn't mean we can't make ourselves believe we are detached from the world because it's in Texas. We need this after being cooped up for so long. Even college was horrible since we had to take classes online! I actually miss the library! Can you imagine that?" Chloe said as she vigorously began filing her nails. "I mean, it is an island, for fuck's sake. So we'll pretend we are sipping fruity drinks from the Bahamas rather than our proverbial backyard—what's the big deal?"

"Perhaps you are right? Thanks to Roger firing me, who knows when I'll have the opportunity or even the money to go on a vacation again? It's not like there are a lot of jobs out there in my field at the moment. There isn't exactly an immense need for lawyers since all the courts had closed during the pandemic. I mean, I could go back to bartending. That's always an option. But I hated the nightlife even back in college."

"Exactly! You don't need a shit job that will lead you to deal with more scum like Roger. And if you ask me, he was a dick to fire you, and you should sue him for harassment or something." Said Zoey as she crossed her arms and formed a pout to emphasize her distaste for the man.

"No. I can either spend my money on a lawyer-friend, and it'll last for only 2 meager moments in Roger's life to feel miserable—or? I can have the trip of a lifetime with all y'all."

"Choose curtain number two! Choose curtain two!" Chloe said, jumping up and down, her mousey brown pin-straight long hair bouncing off her shoulders as she clasped her hands together and widened her excited eyes.

"Girls, I think I've decided. Let's pack our bags!"

They all screamed and formed a group hug around Harper.

"You won't regret this, Harper! I promise." Said Chloe.

"I'm going with the two of you. Of course, I'm going to regret part of this trip. Y'all aren't the best of influence on me. Remember that frat party at the Alpha Sig?"

Both Chloe and Zoey put their heads down.

"In our defense, the guy said it was for charity." Said Chloe.

Harper crossed her arms.

"Since when is giving away a worn bra and panties a charity thing? You should have tried to stop me."

"And in our defense, also? Have you ever tried to stop you? It's not exactly easy, you know." Said Zoey.

"Just make sure I stay away from anything with vodka in it. That sinful sauce always gets me into trouble, and I'll trade the Cosmopolitans in for Mai Tais." Said Harper.

"Oh yes! I want to sip the fruity drinks from a pineapple! That would be fun!" Said Chloe.

Harper headed home to pack a weekend bag, but as she placed each article of clothing into the bag, she wondered if she was making the biggest mistake of her life. She usually never had an issue deciding what to do, but the girls always convinced her to change her mind. Now she was thinking this was one of those reasons.

Her bank account was dwindling to an almost nonexistent status now that she'd been out of work for the last six months. She'd taken a few odd jobs here and there, but nothing was solid because of the pandemic. Even her typical go-to of bartending wasn't a stable paycheck these days because no one was dining in restaurants or bars. Everything was takeout. Going on this trip was probably the silliest thing to do, especially when it meant dipping into her also almost nonexistent 401K.

A knock at her bedroom door broke her from her thoughts, and her mother was at the threshold.

"Hey, enjoy yourself, hun." She said as she handed her a check.

"Mom, what's all of this?"

"I want you to have some fun, and I understand that money is tight for you right now."

"Mom, you don't need to do this. I'm quite capable—"

"Yes—you can support yourself. But you've been moping around the house—not that you could do much about that since there's been a pandemic, but still! It's time to forget about Roger! And who knows? You might run into a lawyer looking for a partner while you are there. It always pays to put your feelers out there."

"But Mom?"

"Don't but Mom me! If you must—consider this an early birthday gift. Your birthday is next month anyway, and 25 is a big milestone. So you should enjoy this time with your friends."

"Yeah, please don't remind me I'll be a quarter of a century year's old, mother."

"Please do not ever utter that phrase again to your vintage mother. She feels old enough without you reminding her."

Harper smiled.

"Thanks, Mom," her mother placed the check into the palm of Harper's hand.

"You know I'm gonna eventually pay you back for this—right?"

"You're my kid, so of course, you will. That doesn't mean I have to accept it back, though. Just do us a favor and have fun. You deserve it."

CHAPTER 3

THE FIRST CLASS TREATMENT

Harper finished packing, was out the door, and headed straight to her friends' Zoey and Chloe's apartment. Within a few brief minutes, the three of them piled into Harper's car for the short trek to Pearl South Padre Island.

Chloe pulled out a brochure of the hotel resort they'd be staying at from her purse.

"I really want to do this sandcastle contest they have. I've got to put that pottery class I took in college to good use, and sandcastles are a good way to hone my carving skills."

"I'm going to get my tan on. To be this gorgeous takes work." Zoey said with a chuckle.

Harper groaned.

"That's hilarious, Zoey."

"What? It's the truth!" She said with a pout forming on her lips.

Harper let out a breath.

"I miss this. It's been a long time since the three of us had time to hang out."

"Yeah, it has been a long time. But that's only because you used to work long ass hours for that son of a bitch narcissist. Honestly, I won't ever understand how you put up with him for that long."

"I don't know either, Zo."

The three pulled into the resort's parking area and quickly hopped out of the car, eyes wide.

"I never imagined it would be this gorgeous! All of Texas is so rural, with wide-open fields and farmland. Never dawned on me it could be so islandy—ya know? I mean, even near the small beach, you've got places like Corpus Christi that make you feel more like you are in small-town USA."

Harper patted Zoey on the shoulder before answering her.

"Yup, and for the next week, the only sound I

want to hear is the beach waves. Let's get checked in and then head to the bar. It's 5 o'clock somewhere!"

"You don't have to tell me that twice." Said Chloe as she tugged on her suitcase and headed towards the resort's entrance. "I'll get us checked in since I'm the one that booked the suite. Couldn't believe they had a business suite for such an awesome price! I mean—I get Covid and all—but lots of people like us are now vaccinated."

Harper shrugged her shoulders.

"People are still scared. I don't blame them."

Harper and Zoey stayed outside the lobby as Chloe headed in. It was only a matter of a few minutes when Chloe flagged them to enter the building so they could get to their suite. They ran into the elevator, and Chloe pushed the penthouse suite button on the elevator keys.

"Whoa! When you said it was a suite, I just assumed it was a business suite." Harper said with widened eyes.

"Oh, it was supposed to be! But there was some mixup where they booked the room we were supposed to have twice on the same night. The flustered girl at the front desk didn't know what to do when I asked for the manager. Turned out the manager—or rather, the resort's owner was right behind her, anyway. When she discovered that the mixup occurred because of my third-party booking, the owner offered us the penthouse for our trouble! Can you imagine our luck? This is going to be awesome! She told me about this party happening tonight, too. I guess they are going to do mixers every Friday and Saturday night for the next several weeks to drum up some business. So this will be extra fun! Can you imagine all the young and hot single men?"

"Holy shit, Chloe! That's fucking amazing!"

"I know, right, Zo? This stroke of luck punched up this trip several notches if you ask me."

The doors opened to a hallway leading to the only door on the entire floor. Chloe opened it with her keycard, and they all walked in with their mouth agape.

"Holy shit! This place is huge!" Harper said as she walked over to the floor-to-ceiling sliding glass doors that overlooked the ocean. She opened the sliders and was greeted by the gentle sounds of the waves crashing on the beach. A warm breeze cradled her face. She inhaled the salty scent that teased her nostrils with one deep breath. "This is the life. And okay, I will admit that I'm glad y'all convinced me to take this trip with you."

"See? I figured you'd admit to the error of your ways sooner or later. We are going to have so much fun! Let's head down to that outdoor bar I saw by the pool area." Chloe said as she pulled out her sun hat and sunglasses from her suitcase.

"You both head down. I'll catch up. I have to change into my bathing suit first." Harper unzipped her suitcase and rummaged through it for her cute gold-toned Victoria's Secret two-piece.

"Don't take too long, Harper! We are hitting the margaritas first, and then Chloe and I are on our mission to bag you a cute cabana boy for this mini-vacation. Because, girl, you need to get laid!"

"Zo!"

"I mean it, Harper! We are finding you a boy-toy because that's exactly what you need to get out of that whole mopy funk you've got going on. You need to forget about Roger."

Harper stuck her tongue out at Zoey before darting into the bedroom she decided to claim as hers for the week. Once the suite door shut, she took a long breath.

I know they mean well, but I don't want to get stuck with a Roger 2.0 on this vacation.

She put on her bikini, a coverup, and donned her favorite white-trimmed, oversized Jessica Simpson sunglasses. And all before she opened the door leading out of the suite so she could meet up with her friends. As she swung the door open, she realized she had forgotten her keycard. She slammed the door and heard a rather large thud on the other end. Harper quickly grabbed the door handle and tried to peek around it to see what made the noise, but there was a bit of resistance to the door. To her horror, a man holding his forehead came into view.

"Oh crap! I am so, so sorry! Normally I open and close the door slowly, but since we are the only room on this floor, I didn't think anybody would be on the other end."

"It's okay. I was just about to knock and ask if you needed anything."

Harper extended her hand as she spoke.

"Oh no, I think we are doing okay, for now, Mr.?"

"Oh! Just call me Colton." He said as he took her hand in his. A warmth immediately washed over her body as his skin made contact with hers.

"Well, Colton," she started as she came out from behind the door. She looked down at his swimsuit uniform and swallowed hard before continuing, "it's, uh, nice to meet you. I'm sorry about hitting you on the forehead. Can I do something to make it up to you? Perhaps buy you a drink?" She swallowed hard again and lowered her head further to the floor.

Heat rushed to her cheeks. She was completely taken aback by this man standing in her doorway. All he was missing was a leaf to cover up his dick, and she'd get down on her knees and worship that man as a god until he came five times for her. To be that gorgeous—and with an eight-pack no less should be considered a mortal sin. But she'd do whatever he wanted for repentance and, or adoration.

"I'm sorry, but I'm on duty—no drinking on the job and all that jazz. I'm the cabana boy. So if you need anything during your stay, just let me know."

"Well, what about when you are off duty?" Her voice came out rushed, something she didn't want. She sounded bothered, and she was if you added the word hot before the bothered. Holding his hand made her stomach flutter in ways she'd forgotten about since high school.

"Um, Miss?"

"Harper! My name is Harper, and I'd love it if you'd join me for a drink after you get off work. I feel horrible about this whole thing, and you did ask if there was anything I needed. Well, giving you a proper apology is, uh," She licked her lips as her eyes glanced south again.

Oh God, he's driving me crazy! Why did he have to wear a bandaid as his cabana boy uniform?

"is what I, I... Desperately want you—I mean," Harper screwed her eyes shut before continuing, "I need you—I mean, to,"

You're screwing up this apology royally, Harper!

A thought of riding his cock until he came five more times rushed through her mind.

Speaking of screwing—how the hell does that dick of his fit in a woman's body? It's ginormous!

"Apologize! Ugh! I'm sorry. Is it hot in here?" She fanned herself. "Um, I'm going down to the bar to cool off. Maybe I'll see you there?"

He knew she was staring at his junk the entire time they talked. The damned bitch he worked for was making his life difficult and all because Blake wanted to get the free show. Clearly, Blake didn't bank on the competition she'd have at the resort. And right now, Colton was happy with the woman staring at him. He didn't think he'd admit that to himself. But this woman who was so adorable, tripping over her words, was the most beautiful woman he'd ever met. Then she bit her lip, and that made his dick hard. He shifted his stance, hoping his cock wouldn't spill out of the tiny fabric.

Her words dripped as quickly as the sweat slid from his brow. She was hot, and his dick ached to be inside her. But he couldn't tell her that. The woman before him was nothing like any other woman he'd ever met. She was sweet and so damned hot.

He knew that if Blake caught him with Harper, she'd have something to say about it, but he honestly didn't care. Something about this woman made him want to scream out the word yes, and repeatedly. His dick strained again against his tight Speedo, and she seemed to enjoy the view, given how her eyes only met his other head once since their conversation started.

Great, just what I need right now. You are giving this Harper chick a free show, so knock it off, dick! Down, boy!

The last thing he wanted to do was come across to her as just another guy looking to get laid.

"I get off at eight." He said to her with a smile

while looking at his hand she still had clasped in hers.

A smile broadened on her gorgeous golden-toned face. She had an earthy essence as she tossed her jet-black, curly hair to one side of her shoulder. Before Colton realized it, he pulled her hand to his lips and brushed the cool skin with a kiss. Her gaze finally looked up at him for the second time in this conversation, and he felt his heart flutter as he locked his eyes on hers. They were a beautiful chocolate brown.

"Oh, that's great! Hopefully, we can meet up." She smiled brightly at him but was still unwilling to let his hand go.

"Um, can I get my hand back?" He finally wound up saying to her after a few brief moments.

"Right! Sorry!" Her tone came out breathy as she released her grip. His hand went cold the instant she broke the hold between them, and a pang came over his chest. It was almost as if his entire being mourned from the absence of her touch.

"I'll look for you once I'm off."

"I'd like that."

His wolf instantly came to the forefront of his mind. Before he could dial back the beast, his hand snaked around her waist, pulling her close to him.

"I'd really like to kiss you, Harper." He could hear his wolf growling in a low, guttural tone as her eyes flicked to his lips.

His human half kept trying to reel the wolf in. He was usually pretty good with keeping that half of him tame, even though he hadn't been a shifter for that long. In the beginning, he had an awful time. Blake didn't make things easy. It was hard controlling his temper when she was around. But with other things—like sex with Blake—his feelings were easily kept squarely inside his pants.

What's so different now?

This seemed wrong on so many levels. Especially since Colton vowed to himself when he started this job that he'd never engage or pursue the guests romantically. And according to Blake, she swung both ways. So he didn't want to give Blake any ideas about a threesome because he was sure that thought crossed Blake's mind on more than one occasion. He was a one-woman guy, and there was nothing Blake could do to change his mind on the subject.

Harper, though? She surprised him because she was so different from any woman he'd ever met. The glances into his eyes that symbolized sheer attraction were enough for him alone to want to be this crazy with her. But she also had a cuteness about her when she stumbled over her words. Harper's hand traveled up his back and into his hair. The sensation of her perfectly manicured nails sent waves of electricity to his cock, now pressed against her inner thigh.

She then did the unthinkable—at least to him, it was. She stood on the tips of her toes and kissed his lips. Currents of heat, excitement, and anticipation of pleasure coursed through his body all at once. Never in all of his life had he been with a girl that made the first move. Sure—he asked if he could kiss her, but her reaction was so much different from any of the other women he'd been with before.

He caressed her back as she plunged her tongue into his mouth and explored every inch. She was such a good kisser, making him wonder how her mouth would feel wrapped around his cock. His dick twitched at the thought because it would feel like a divine intervention as she sucked his cock until he came into her mouth. His wolf made a soft moan, and then his hands glided down to cup her ass. It was perfectly round, making him want to pull her closer to his waist as he caressed each tight globe.

He deepened the kiss and assaulted her lips as she pawed at his bare chest and moaned over his mouth. The vibration made him thicker with need.

He thrust his cock into her sex as she wrapped her legs around his waist. She felt so good--even with thin fabric separating them. He continued to tease her, sucked on her bottom lip until he felt her palms on his chest pushing him away. Her body slid down his, and that sensation made him mourn the loss of her touch. A shiver ran up his spine as she continued to put distance between the two of them.

"I'll definitely look for you after you get off work." She said as she beamed from ear to ear before heading towards the elevator. It opened as soon as she touched the button. She placed her hand on the open door and looked toward him.

"Do you need a ride down?"

He wanted more than anything to give her the ride of her life, but he couldn't. Not yet. She deserved so much more than a quickie. That thought made him say something he'd never spoken to a woman before.

"No, Harper. I'm the hired help, and I have the freight elevator."

Her smile turned slightly downward.

"Oh, that's a shame." She said before she popped her body into the cart.

The elevator door shut, and she immediately let out a breath she didn't realize she'd been holding in. Once the elevator had passed a couple of floors, she let out a screech.

"Oh, my God! I practically boned that guy in the hallway! What was I thinking?" She let out a sigh while running a hand through her thick locks. "He's so damned hot, though!"

Harper touched her lips, hoping the burn he left on them would last a little longer. She'd never been this bold with a guy before—ever. But something about Colton made her inner diva want to pop out and take over.

She had hoped he'd ride down the elevator with her because she wanted him to kiss her again as they descended to the lobby. Breaking away from him was more brutal than with any other man she'd ever been with. And that made her wonder if she could trust herself alone with Colton. She had barely learned of his name for five seconds, and her hands were all over him. She wasn't giving him a good impression. All she was doing was showing him she wasn't into a committed relationship. And that was the exact opposite of what she wanted with this guy.

Hmmm... Colton had the body of a Greek god, though! I need to talk to the girls about him.

Usually, she kept her crushes to herself unless they turned out to be more than that. But something in her wanted to tell the world that she had the hots for this guy, and boy, did she have it bad. She'd never been the jealous type where she laid claim to her men, but with Colton, she wanted to make sure Chloe and Zoey knew to back off. That thought alone worried her because if she was falling this hard and this fast, that wouldn't be good. Not when she didn't know if Colton would turn out to be another Roger. Harper had to play it cool with him if he met up with her for drinks later. She would not get her heart stomped on again. Especially when she was on vacation, and this was more likely a fling.

CHAPTER 4

ONE WEEK OF FUN

"Girl! What took you so long? We nearly finished our first round!" Zoey asked as Harper approached their loungers.

Harper couldn't shake her grin as they handed her a salt-rimmed margarita on the rocks.

"I've seen that look before! That's a record! You haven't even gotten your first drink on, and you've already met a guy—haven't you?"

"Not so fast, Zo. I'm only going for a drink with the guy, and I'm taking him for one because I hit him in the face with the door to our penthouse."

"Likely excuse!" Zoey said with a cackle.

"No, really! I felt bad!" Harper took a sip of her drink before placing it on the side table and sat on one of the lounger chairs next to Chloe and Zoey.

"Okay, I'll give you that, but what's he like? Something's got you all giddy, so he's clearly hot —right?"

Harper caught a glimpse of Colton over Zoey's shoulder as he left the hallway near the elevators. He was rounding the bar and well within sight for both girls to see him in his god-like glory.

"See for yourself. Personally, I think Colton's Greek-god hot, and just calling him a hottie doesn't do him justice." She motioned her chin over Zoey's shoulder. The girls turned their heads slightly in the direction Harper gave them, careful not to draw attention to themselves as they stared.

The girls' mouths were slightly agape as the man smiled in Harper's direction.

"He's pure flames, Harper."

"Shut up, Chlo! He's gorge with a capital freakin' G. The fuck, Harper! How'd you score a babe like that so fast? The dude doesn't have a six-pack—he's got more like an eight-pack. His sexy V is super toned, too. I mean, damn! Hello, tall, dark, and sexy." Zoey said as she licked her lips for a more dramatic effect.

"I think the two of you need to slow your roll." Harper mouthed to them as Colton sauntered over to them. "He's mine because I saw him first."

"Hello, ladies. Welcome to the Pearl South Padre Island Resort and Spa. My name is Colton, and if you need anything, please don't hesitate to ask." Colton said with a smile directed straight at Harper.

"I'm thirsty," Zoey licked her lips, and the smack rang above the waves.

"Yeah, I'm totally parched myself." Chloe chuckled and bit her lip.

"I can grab you, ladies, a drink." Colton never took his eyes off of Harper. "What is it you desire?"

Harper shifted herself on her lounger as her face flushed. This man knew what buttons to push to get her hot and bothered again. The girls merely cackled at her unease.

"Something tells me, Harper, that you are in the mood for a Colt—"

Harper elbowed Zoey before she could finish her sentence.

"What? Don't tell me you don't drink beer." Zoey said with a broad smile while rubbing her upper arm. "I mean, seriously!"

"We'd love a round of margaritas, Colton, but I can get them myself."

"Nonsense, Harper! Y'all relax, and I'll be back in a jiff with those."

Harper watched Colton saunter from their

lounge chairs towards the bar. His backside swayed to imaginary music in a perfect, fluid rhythm, and his feet almost looked as if they didn't touch the floor. Once he was out of earshot, she glared at her girls.

"Would the two of you quit it? I'm only taking him for a drink because I literally ran into him with the door. That's all!"

"Oh, get off it, Harper! You've got the hots for him, so don't try to deny it!"

"I do not deny anything, Zoe! I just don't want you making this out to be something it isn't."

"What are you yapping on about, Harper?"

"We are here for a week and to have fun—that's it, Zoe." Harper retorted.

"No—we," Zoey started as she motioned a hand between her and Chloe before continuing, "are here to have fun. You, my dear, are here to get laid. Because that is one sure-fire way to forget that dick Roger, capisci?"

Harper glared and crossed her arms.

"I'm not sleeping with him for the sake of sleeping with someone, Zoe."

"Harper, I get it's been a while since you've been in the dating game, but dear, you don't need to find out if he's dating material to get a fling going. I mean, come on! The guy was coming onto you like the Fast and the Furious. You can't tell me he's not used to having flings at this resort. He's the cabana boy, for Christ's sake. He must have slept with a girl in each state by now. And by the way, girl, if you weren't considering tapping that—I will!"

Harper's face flushed again.

"First off, he's not a piece of ass, Zoe! Second, hands-off because I saw him first—I mean it."

Zoey's brows furrowed.

"I'm only kidding. I want you to have some fun because I'm your friend. And as a friend, I'm going to give you some advice about the cabana boy—don't fall for him—just enjoy his company. No strings, Harper! It's better that way because I don't want you heartbroken."

Harper let out a long breath.

"I know you are right about him. But I just can't help feeling the way I do." Harper grabbed her drink and downed it in one quick sip.

"Wait! Girl! Are you getting jelly over what I said in jest? Girl! You know I'm all about girl code, so I'm sorry if I made you feel like I wasn't."

"I know you are, Zoe. It's just I really like him, and that makes me nervous. I don't know if I trust myself alone with him."

Chloe rested her palm on Harper's arm.

"If you are this physically attracted to him before you even go on a date, then I wouldn't worry about trusting yourself. It's passion in the purest sense. Just enjoy the ride this week and move on."

"Yeah, I know there is a difference between like and love."

"Spitting or swallowing, you mean," Zoey giggled and winked.

The three were in full-on cackling mode when Colton came over with their drinks.

"Thanks, Colton," Harper said as she handed him her credit card. Her face flushed again as a thought about her lips around his cock flashed before her.

Colton put out his palm toward her card.

"No need to run a tab. The drinks are on the house."

His voice had a sharp sound to it. Harper narrowed her brows at the difference in his tone. He hadn't been that cold to her while she was practically dry-humping him at the penthouse minutes ago.

"Ladies, welcome! Colton is right. The drinks are on the house for this evening. I felt bad about the mixup with your room and want to make it up to all of y'all."

"Well, thanks, ma'am, but I insist on paying because you've already done right by us with upgrading the suite. So please, put these on my tab." Harper said as she flashed her card at the tall women standing before them, practically interrupting Colton. The fair-haired runway-looking model was dressed in a gorgeous two-piece that put Harper's to shame. Harper—at least when she had a good job—spent money on clothes. It was her one splurge in life. But she'd never drop over a grand on a Tom Ford bikini!

"I'm not a ma'am." The woman said with a chuckle.

"Sorry. It's just a form of respectful lingo we use here in Texas. I meant nothing by it."

"Clearly, we've gotten a bit off on the wrong foot. My name is Blake Evans, and I am the Pearl South Padre Island Resort and Spa owner." She said as she extended her hand out to Harper. "I do hope you will enjoy your stay. Do you plan on coming to the dance party tonight? It's at the bar, and all the singles will be here."

"We were planning on it! Colton, will you be there, too?" Zoey asked.

Harper shot her a glare.

"Colton?" Blake said as she slinked an almost pasty, paper-thin arm around Colton's broad shoulders. "He's part of my crew." A steely smile formed on her lips before continuing, "So, of course, he will be there."

Harper's eyes darted to the woman's dainty hand that caressed his peck muscle while she spoke. Harper's eyes sharpened at the gesture.

Clearly, he's got a girlfriend. What a prick.

Harper lowered her head and played with her fingernails, pretending to appear disinterested. With the woman, it seemed to have worked. But once she raised her eyes back towards Colton, she saw a riddled look on his face. He cleared his throat, gazed down at the floor, and stepped away from the Barbie doll next to him.

"I'm always around if you need me." His voice was almost a whisper.

Blake caressed his cheek.

"That's my boy, always eager to please the guests." Her hand traveled down to his chest again. He flinched and stepped away again from her.

The fuck?

"Ladies, I'll be here if you need me, but I hope you and my boss will understand something. I have other things to attend to before the mixer tonight."

He didn't even look up before turning on his heel and walking towards the poolside waterfall section.

"I'm sorry, ladies. I'm trying to get him to be more congeal with the guests. It's hard for him to flirt in this atmosphere like he should—especially in front of me. You understand—right?"

Harper looked down. She didn't want this woman thinking she bested her. It was sad, though, because Harper really thought Colton liked her, especially after that kiss. But? It turned out he was just another Roger. The one thing she promised herself not to go after during this trip. Absolutely no Roger 2.0, and she clearly broke that promise to herself now that she saw with her own eyes that Colton was fucking his boss.

"Of course we understand. We didn't realize the two of you were dating." Said Zoey as she sported a fake smile.

"We have for a while. I'm honestly surprised Colton hasn't proposed yet." Blake cackled and then turned on her heel and walked away.

"You guys can go to the dance party and have some fun. I'm going to turn in early." Harper played with the straw and ice cubes in her drink.

"Harper! You need to come out with us tonight. Have some fun. Go on that date."

"It's not a date—clearly, it's not since he's fucking the resort owner."

"I wouldn't be so sure about that, Harper. He wanted nothing to do with the woman—couldn't you see he was trying to get away from her?"

"I don't need another Roger in my life."

"Babe—he's not Roger. Just do us a favor and come with us tonight. Buy the guy a drink and see what he has to say for himself. If he turns out to be a lying sack of shit, you'll have plenty of other guys to flirt with at the dance party tonight."

Harper was about to protest when Colton appeared from across the poolside. He locked his eyes onto hers and began heading toward her. But Blake Barbie Doll Evans stopped him, and she draped an arm around him, and he quickly pulled it off. His face flushed in heat, his eye fixated on Harper again, and his mouth spat out inaudible words she couldn't make out.

"You know what, girls, you are right. Plenty of fish in the sea. Let's go get ready for this shindig." Said Harper as she glanced away from the two of them.

"That's the spirit!" Said Chloe. "And don't worry,

babe, from the looks of it, Blake doesn't stand a chance at keeping him—even if she's actually dating him—which I honestly doubt she is. The girl was trying too hard to convince us. You know what I'm saying?"

CHAPTER 5

THE DOG HOUSE

"You will not engage those girls at the dance party. Do you understand me, Colton?"

Blake palmed his cheek and guided his gaze back towards her once she noticed his eyes darting towards the three of them as she spoke to him at the bar.

"Absolutely no mate of mine will be with other women unless I'm up for a threesome. And if we have a threesome, I'm picking the girl."

"I am not, nor will I ever be, your mate, Blake. We've been through this before. Now, if you'll excuse me, I have drinks to serve to those girls. My job is to please everyone at the resort—those were your words."

"That's not how the mate bond works, and you know it. I claimed you. You're mine, and that's the end of it since I'm your Alpha Queen. And as far as those girls go—yes, serve them alcohol, so they are pliable for the Omegas."

"I'm not your property, bitch! Stop acting all batshit."

He could feel the heat welling inside of him, and suddenly it rushed to his ears and cheeks. Colton wanted to pummel the brick wall in front of him. But he decided against it since the normals, as he liked to call them, would notice the large hole in the wall and wonder how any ordinary man could have that kind of strength. Being a shifter sucked sometimes, and this was proving to be one of those times. He took in a breath to calm himself before he continued. "And as soon as I figure out how to break this sadistic bond you made between us, I will rid myself of you for good."

"You wouldn't survive more than five seconds out there in the big, bad world. Who will hire a man with a temper large enough to destroy an entire building with a single punch? Or did you forget about the hotel room you trashed when I first turned you? You still owe me money for the repairs, and you're lucky I haven't docked your pay for that.

So face it—you've no choice but to stay here with me because I'm the one who keeps your head calm and collected."

She ran a finger down his bare chest. Her finger felt like a dagger piercing his skin with each word she uttered. Part of him wished she were talking nonsense. But it had taken him time to control his rage. Sadly, she tended to make it spike because of how much he loathed what she made him into.

He hated to admit it, but she was right. He had a temper at the beginning that was hard to control. Lately, the anger seemed to subside a little. It was easier for him to be around the normals, but he was still afraid of what might happen if he didn't have the pack around him as a safety net. He let out a sigh. Which was something he knew he shouldn't do in front of Blake because it was a sign of defeat. He did it more to let out the breath he'd been holding in the whole time they'd been talking. Colton couldn't let her get his goat this time. She had so many times before because everything about her infuriated him at this point. He had no idea why he was stupid enough to date her. She wasn't overly pretty—not compared to Harper, anyway. Blake's smug smiles were a definite turnoff. They made her look like Jezebel herself, whereas Harper's genuine smile could light up a room. Another smug look wiped over Blake's face, reminding him once more that she forced him to turn over more than his humanity. She stole his soul, too.

"I've got the pool maintenance to finish before this dance party and these drinks to serve. So if you have nothing pressing, I need to get going." He said as he backed away from her and balled his fist.

"Very well, but remember—I don't want you flirting with those three girls. I have plans to fix them up with the Omegas. The brunette you had your eye on is stunning, and I think she'll be a favorite of the pack. They'll surely pass her around with all the boys more than once." Blake cackled. "I'm going to ensure our bartender is fully stocked with potions to add to the drinks tonight. We don't want any of these girls to catch on to the fact that they're here to entertain us shifters—not the other way around." She turned on her heel and walked off.

He sighed as soon as she was out of his sightline.

Crap! Now, what am I going to do about tonight?

A tap on his shoulder broke him from his thoughts.

"Dude, it's not that easy. To help those girls, you first need to stop talking to yourself."

"What are you talking about, Marcus?"

Colton's brows knitted as he asked his friend and co-worker.

"You do realize Blake can read your thoughts—right? That's how she figured out you would go over to flirt with that Harper girl."

"How did you know her name was Harper?"

"Because I can pick up on your thoughts, too. It's a wolf thing. Well, actually, it's more of a pack thing. She can only read your thoughts if she's near you. But while she's down in the basement, she can't, and that's why I came to you now. But you still should be careful. If you don't want her ever reading your thoughts, Raffe and I can teach you how to block her. Head over to my room in about five minutes. And whatever you do—do not think about what I just said. She'll figure it out, and then we'll all be in her proverbial dog house. The best thing to do now is to think about fantasy football stats. She hates that and will tune you out within seconds of invading your headspace."

Colton nodded and then made his way to the brothers' room. It opened within seconds of him knocking at the door, and Raffe greeted him.

"Don't say a word. Just come on in and drink this."

Colton took the mug from Raffe's hand and drank what he presumed was tea. The contents smelled earthy but seemed rather bland as he took his first sip. He finished the mug and handed it back to Raffe.

"Good! Now we can talk freely without her reading your mind." Raffe said with a smile.

"What was that?"

Before Raffe could answer, Marcus walked through the door.

"Blake isn't the only one that knows a thing or two about potions. That one we gave you will last for 24 hours, and that should be just enough time for you to master a simple binding spell. You'll need to say the spell at midnight and repeat it three times for it to work. And obviously, you will have to do this while the potion still influences her, just so you can say the spell in your head."

"But won't she find it odd that she suddenly can't read my thoughts?"

"That's the beauty of this binding spell—she won't have the slightest clue."

"Well, that and this." Said Marcus as he held out a chain with a dark solitary stone on it.

"I've seen the two of you wearing those all the time, and I figured it was a family thing."

"It's an obsidian crystal that keeps her nasty ass out of our heads."

"Can I refuse her as a mate once I say this spell?"

"Yes. You'll have the power within you to go rogue. But with the way you've been able to resist her lately, her hold isn't as strong as she'd hoped. Of course, denouncing her can take months. This spell will speed things along for you, and you can leave whenever you'd like."

"Why didn't the two of you do the same? I mean, not that she is out of your head—don't you want to leave?"

Raffe shrugged his shoulders before answering.

"We want to keep the normals safe. That's why we've stayed on for so long. We don't want anyone being turned against their will. Before you, Blake was reasonable. She allowed none of the Omegas to turn someone against their will. But with the pandemic—she's been desperate to keep the pack satisfied."

"So is that why the Omegas never seem to find a mate at these dance parties? You two are the ones keeping all the girls safe?"

"That would be why."

"I'm glad there're guys like you on my side, then."

"Okay, here's the spell, and remember, it has to be said at midnight for it to work."

Raffe pressed a small piece of paper into Colton's hand. Colton shoved the piece of paper inside the tool belt he had dangled around his waist. His new uniform not only lacked material to cover his junk, but it also lacked pockets.

"Thanks, guys!" Colton said before he went through the door.

"And don't worry, we will keep an eye on all three girls tonight. I get she wants you to stay away from them, but we have ways of keeping Blake distracted so you can say hi to that Harper girl. We know you like her. That was blatant when we heard your thoughts about kissing her. So just leave every-thing to us."

"Thanks, guys, but given what Blake pulled this afternoon, that ship may have sailed."

"Nonsense! If there's anyone who can smooth talk—it's you, Colton."

"I may understand how to talk with our fearless Blake, but Harper isn't going to be that easy, Raffe.

First, I want to sweet talk Harper—not tell her off."
Colton chuckled.

"At the very least—try," Raffe said as he patted Colton on the shoulder.

"I will."

CHAPTER 6

PREDICTIONS ARE A TRICKY THING

"Chloe, I don't want to argue about this. It was a mistake for me to come here. I'm clearly not over Roger, and as far as a fling goes? Well, I put my eggs in a basket I had no business putting them in." Harper said with a sigh.

Zoey placed a palm on Harper's shoulder.

"I don't think he is a bad guy. He seemed really nice when he was talking to us alone."

Harper turned to Zoey.

"Zoey, how can you say that? Blake was all over him. No, he's a dog—just like Roger, and I should have never kissed him like," Her voice trailed for a moment as she swallowed, "like he was the last man on Earth."

"Oh, please! He wanted nothing to do with her.

Can't you see it, Harper? The guy has the hots for you, and his boss is jealous of how gorgeous you are. Honestly, if you want the guy, you'd win. There's not much of a fight because Blake isn't half the woman you are. He'd be yours for however long you want him." Said Chloe as she dabbed some concealer on her face.

"I don't need more drama around me, and something tells me this one will bring a lot of it into my life."

"God, Harper! Was it your fault the bitch Roger cheated on you with had made a scene at work? Let me answer that for you before you try! No, of course not!"

Harper let out a sigh.

"So not the point, Chloe, and you know it."

"No, the point is you let yourself get hurt over a guy you just met. This guy is supposed to be a mere distraction from the reality you left at home. Face it, Harper, you aren't great about letting things go."

"Point taken, Zoey, but I still don't feel like going. With my mood, I'd be a party pooper. So maybe just the two of you should go."

"Please come?" Chloe said with a pouty face.

"Okay, tell you what. Let me take a shower, and

I'll meet the two of you down there. If both of you are right, then making Colton sweat is good?"

"Of course, it is a good thing!"

Harper smiled and turned on the shower as her two friends made it out of the suite. As the steam billowed in the room, Harper removed her bikini and hopped in. Beads of water pooled on her shoulders. The heat relaxed all the tension built up the minute Blake introduced herself to Harper.

How the fuck can I be so stupid? He's got a girl!

In the back of her mind, a voice she'd always assumed was her mother, the voice of reason, formed the response she'd just given to her friends moments ago. She wasn't sure why she agreed to meet them downstairs. All the signs were pointing to staying away from Colton. Still, something seemed to guide her, some other voice that wasn't from her mother.

You are not stupid. He is your mate.

Harper let out a sigh as she lathered her hair. She did not know why that thought came over her, but she wasn't about to figure it all out now. As the water rinsed her head of hair, the voice crept in again.

He is your mate.

She now doubted her sanity. How could a guy

she was clearly only in lust with be her mate? What's more? Why was she calling him a mate in the deep throes of her mind? She'd never call someone a mate—she wasn't British. Nor was she naïve enough to think someone would fall so madly in love with her that they'd want to be with her for forever. That shit only happened in fairytales. At least that's what her dad always told her. As she got older, she realized he said it so she wouldn't become disillusioned with the idea of love.

Not that she was awe-struck with Roger— though her friends assumed she was. She knew he'd hurt her because all men did at some point in her life. Every boyfriend, her brother, and even her father had let her down in the past. None of it was a surprise to her anymore. She could perceive the outcome of a relationship before the kiss goodnight on date one. Harper chalked that up to being psychic. She knew at least that much, but the accuracy she exhibited frightened her. Most psychics she knew guest-starred on those daytime talk shows and were constantly called out for being fakes because they were 70% accurate. But not Harper. She always saw the breakup coming 100% of the time.

She hated that side of herself. The ability always

scared her. Once she became less afraid of her powers, she tried to figure out a timeline for when said breakup would occur. But no matter how hard she tried, she never seemed to pinpoint a timeline. She sucked with predicting time. Which if she was honest? It probably had something to do with math —she was sure of that because she sucked at math, too.

All she wanted was to feel something real with a guy. And each time she kissed one, she knew the ultimate demise of the budding relationship. Nothing ever felt real because of that. And it even had her wonder if she was programmed to seek out the losers just to keep on this perpetual hamster wheel of hell with dating without a genuine connection.

She tried her hardest to perceive a future with Colton while under the showerhead, and her brain hit a dark, blank wall.

This is a first! WTF?

She'd always seen an outcome with every guy that walked into her life. Why was Colton a blank slate? Could she have possibly just lost her mojo? It wasn't uncommon; she had heard of psychics losing their gifts. But usually, it was because they had done something to lose them, like closing themselves off from everyone.

Did I do it to myself? Am I really that hung up on Roger?

She struggled to imagine a life without her skills of fortune-telling. Harper was always good at it and had been relying on it to make most of her early adult life decisions. Her father didn't exactly encourage this behavior—but he didn't exactly denounce it either. In fact, he'd gone so far as to give her a deck of cards for her birthday. The deck was old, lacked all 4 queens, and looked like it came from a foreign country.

"These were your great-great grandmother's. Open them!"

She slid the deck out of the casing of red silk and saw that it looked like an ordinary deck of playing cards.

"Dad, what is this?" She asked as her brows knitted.

"It's great-great grandma's tarot deck. She used it to do tarot readings on the boat to kill time while they sailed to America."

"Okay?" Her voice came out more like a state-ment than a question as she slipped the deck back into the silk pouch.

Her father held her hand.

"Hun, I didn't mean to snub you with a gift. If you'd rather I get you some jewelry instead, I can. It's just—" His voice trailed with his eyes, and she witnessed him swallowing hard at his statement.

"But what, Dad? Am I a fucked up version of Sabrina the Teen Witch or something? Is that what this is all about?"

His gaze met hers again.

"Uh? Something like that?"

That was the last thing she heard from him. The completely last conversation they had before the man went into coronary arrest. Before the ambulance arrived, her father was already gone. Not that she didn't try her damnedest to revive him with the CPR training she learned, but even those kinds of practical gifts couldn't save her father.

Roger—at least, she thought—was supportive when she was caregiving for her father. But he fucking sucked with everything else. He often blamed her for being too distant while caring for her father. And it was always when she was administering meds, and she needed her complete concentration for that. He could be such a douche canoe with being selfish. Who was she kidding—he was most definitely a douche canoe. Plain and simple.

And once her father passed, Roger was even worse. He assumed her father would leave some of his estate—not that it was much, but it could be a nice nest egg for both her and him. She wasn't sure what would possess Roger to think he'd get a stock in her father's estate. Especially since her mother would get the house and life insurance policy at the very least.

They'd only been engaged for a couple of months, yet Roger assumed her dad would write him into the will. It was the most bizarre thing to Harper. After that, Roger kept pressuring her to have a talk with her mother about selling the home she grew up in. He kept arguing that the house was too big for her mother to maintain on her own. Thankfully, she caught Roger cheating around when he began pressuring her, making it much easier for her to kick him to the curb.

Perhaps it's good that I don't see an end in sight with Colton?

She let out a sigh and turned off the water.

Who the fuck am I kidding? He'll be like all the rest. I'm just fooling myself with that little 'He's Your Mate' thing going on in the back of my mind.

She pulled on one of the clubbing outfits she had brought along. It was very sparkly, full of bling, and hugged all of her assets well. The shimmering gold mini was just what she needed to hold Colton's attention and away from that bitch named Blake.

She sucked in a breath while realizing that her friends were right. Colton was not Roger. Roger made no attempts in the end to hide his cheating. And it became abundantly clear that he no longer had feelings for Harper because he devoted all of his energy to the other woman. Colton, though, seemed different. She just hoped that different didn't mean that Harper was now *the other woman* in Colton's eyes.

She gave herself another once over in the mirror before heading down to meet with her gal pals and hopefully Colton.

CHAPTER 7

WINE AND MOONLIT NIGHTS

When Colton finally got off of his shift, he looked around for Harper. Versions of tiny white lies ran through his mind as he tried to figure out the best one to tell Harper because of the spell. With Harper, it would be far easier to come up with something than it would be for Blake. He hoped that bitch wouldn't follow him around all night, but with Blake, there was no telling what she'd do. Even saying to her something as final as he was turning in, she'd construe as him wanting to sleep with her. As he searched the crowd for Harper, his eyes settled on Marcus. He walked over to see if either he or Raffe had spotted the girls.

"Hey, Marc! Have you seen—"

"Harper? No, I haven't seen her at all, but the other two are over there."

Marcus pointed over at the corner of the bar where the two girls were, and they appeared to be looking out for Harper as well. He headed over to them when Blake came into view.

"How about you and I head over to the bar for a drink? I understand you just got off of work."

Blake caressed his shoulder as she cooed out her question to him.

"No."

"What do you mean, no?" she crossed her arms over her chest and narrowed her brows.

"I, I still have some stuff to finish—"

"Ms. Evans?" A familiar voice came from behind Colton's back.

Blake shot a look over Colton's shoulder. She made a clucking sound with her tongue before responding.

"What is it, Marcus?"

"The bartender said he's running out of potion —I mean—drink mixes. He asked me to find you since the basement stock is low as well."

"Son of a bitch! Am I the only one that knows how to do anything around here?" Blake stormed off towards the tabletops by the bar where the bartender was serving a few drinks to some giddy girls.

"Thanks, Marc! Let me go warn the girls about the drinks." Colton said as soon as Blake was out of earshot.

"No! You can't! If they don't drink, Blake will get suspicious. It's best if you let Raffe and I hand out the drinks to them—this way, we all know they aren't spiked with god knows what kind of mojo."

"Okay, but I should at least ask them where Harper is."

"Again, no. Blake is already on your ass. It's best to take care of the other girls around the bar area, and Raffe and I will tend to your lady friends. Blake doesn't suspect us of anything, so it'll be easier for us to be inconspicuous with their drinks. Plus, Blake won't care if we flirt with them."

"Noted. Okay. You get I don't like this—but you are right. I'll start making the rounds with the other girls here at the resort to make sure their drinks are only spiked with alcohol."

"Good, and don't forget about what you need to do at midnight."

"I know. I won't forget," Colton said as he tapped the front pocket of his Dockers. He was so glad to be out of that stupid Speedo. Lord knows how many of the girls would be all over him if he had to wear it after hours. At least Blake was sensible enough to allow him to change out of uniform. But given how possessive she'd been all day, she probably did it so no one else would flirt with him.

It grew later in the evening, and Colton still didn't see any sign of Harper. He was getting worried because she had seemed so happy wanting to buy him a drink. Of course, that was until Blake ruined everything for him this afternoon. His heart ached in his chest, a sensation he wasn't accustomed to—at least with women he'd dated. He muttered a silent prayer to the deity he hadn't prayed to since childhood for a chance to make things right with Harper.

Colton learned rather quickly that Blake was the jealous type when they were dating. She was obsessive about calling and texting him at least 10 times while he was working. At first, he assumed Blake was just abusing her power of owning the resort. But when she shadowed him while he was working the bar and constantly draped an arm around him in front of the customers, he knew better. As usual, he'd been thinking with his other head when Blake first came on to him. She was a gorgeous piece of ass, and that was the only criteria he needed to go on a date with a girl. Like always, he planned on just having a one-night stand with her because she was the boss, and dating the boss would become complicated in too many ways. He didn't enjoy referring to himself as a player, but as far as a woman was concerned? He most likely was.

Sex only meant one thing to him—it meant he wasn't completely numb. If his dick was still working, then life was grand, and he was living the dream. But he wasn't stupid. He understood he hurt a lot of women because many of them figured he was kidding when Colton told them he wasn't serious dating material. When the phone call would come the next day from a woman who didn't get it, he seemed to die a little more as the numbness continued to encroach around his heart.

The ironic thing about all of it was the fact he related to vampires. If the bitchiest werewolf that he'd ever met did not bite him, he'd assume the life of the undead. Or at least the metaphysical poet equivalent he studied in college when he could afford classes. He set up a lot of boundaries with people to hide the death within him. And he got pretty good at telling women the boundaries he kept in place to protect what little of a heart he had left. Of course, they weren't really boundaries. Actually, they weren't even walls, either. He had a fortress and a moat around what little he still had inside him to protect. At first, he had this set up because of a woman he'd dated in college. He thought she was going to be the love of his life. He was even ring shopping by the time their six-month dating anniversary came up their senior year of college. Genevieve Kalma was his everything until the day they graduated, and she left. She left him a text telling him her father had died and she had to take over the family business. At the time, he couldn't understand why she left, which was why he blocked his heart from any other woman. But once that bitch turned him, Genevieve showed up in Texas looking for him. Turned out her family business was being a hunter. It took little for Colton to convince her he would never hurt a human being, and probably because she was dating a werewolf named Tarquin at the time. Colton was grateful for Genevieve's compassion because, after becoming a monster, he wanted nothing sweet to enter his dark hell. He feared the pure innocence of any woman would shrivel up and die in his darkness.

Unfortunately, he wound up in bed with a lot of insecure batshit crazy women in his life. Blake was the last straw in the batshit universe. It was almost as if he were a magnet that attracted every crazy woman or monster of the night. Colton had his fill of psycho bitches, even before his mom died, and he didn't desire to go down that path again. Once Colton's mom died, he really had no heart left to get serious with a woman. His mom and Genevieve were the only women that meant anything to him. He watched cancer suck the life out of his mom's strong will, taking her quickly because it was a vicious killer that he could now relate to. As a were-wolf, he could rip apart organs just as cancer could.

No amount of time would have been enough with his mother, but he had told cancer to go fuck itself on more than one occasion under his breath while he took care of her. Genevieve was there with him through most of the darkest times with his mom, offering support in the best ways. Once his mom passed, she left Colton, her only child, every-thing she owned. And according to the lawyer, it was a lot. Enough for Colton to live off of for four full years and still have enough for a nest egg to grow for later in his life. The will reading was around the time of his six-month anniversary with Genevieve, and having the money to afford a ring outright was all he needed to look. Money never came easy for him or even his mother. They were always saving for that proverbial *rainy day*. And frankly, when the time came to pay all the bills, he was glad she'd saved as much as she did. The money she saved and invested not only paid the few bills she'd left behind but also the funeral as well.

With what remained, he took the time he needed to reflect on his life now that the two girls in his life had left him. The illness may have been quick, but Colton dropped out of his master's degree program to care for her. It was a small price to pay to care for her. Looking back, he would do that for her in a heartbeat all over again and twice on Sunday if given a chance. He loved her that much.

Years passed before he even realized that he had spent four years living breath by breath, and when the money was depleting, Coloton realized he needed to pay his own bills. Not that he had a lot of them. Just utilities, food, and taxes. There was no mortgage on the house, so that made things a little easier. When the job came up at the resort, he thought it would be great. He could get a tan and talk to pretty women all day. It solved getting close to another woman without having to. But once Blake sank her teeth into him, all bets were off the table.

She had told him he was strictly her eye candy, and Colton didn't realize what she meant until it was too late. By that point, she already bit him and claimed him as hers. Colton thought the whole thing was strange. He was horrified she bit him, but he couldn't in his wildest dreams believe he'd become a werewolf from her bite on the crux of his neck. And how could a human being own another? And why would a woman say that to a man? Hadn't they, as women, been abused enough? Why retaliate? Especially with a man that had the utmost respect for women. When he turned into a werewolf after the first full moon, he knew what she had done to him and why. She wanted him as her bitch.

The whole werewolf lifestyle had him scratching his head as Blake kept telling him he had to submit to her. But he wasn't having any of that if he could help it.

Colton never submitted to anyone in life. It wasn't his style. He was the type of person to do what he wanted and when he wanted. That's the main reason he asked if he could kiss Harper. He wanted to—God, did he want to! And nothing was going to stop him if she said yes. She was hot! Who wouldn't want to kiss her? And since he wasn't dating Blake, he didn't need her permission to do so. They weren't involved. And that's what made him wonder why Blake kept pushing for this whole wolfy-claimed bullshit. He didn't feel any different towards Blake. In fact, his feelings went south the minute she bit him. He now hated her with conviction.

Harper, though? She was entirely different. He didn't exactly take the time to get to know her before he started making out with her, but he could tell that there was something different about her. She was genuine because every fiber of his being told him this. She didn't have an err about herself as Blake did. And she was fun to be around. Sadly, he seemed to have learned more from Harper in the few minutes he was making out with her than Colton did in the entire season he had known Blake and started working at the Pearl South Padre.

All he really learned about Blake was that she was an extremely jealous person, and she had no idea what personal space was. That was pretty sad, indeed. And even compared to other girls that he had one-night stands with, he knew less about Blake than any of the rest of them.

He searched around the bar once more, and there was still no sign of Harper. He let out a sigh while glancing at his phone. It was a quarter to midnight, and he had to move away from the party if he had any plans of saying the spell undisturbed. There was a quiet cabana that no one ever rented because it hadn't been renovated in a long while. So he decided that was the best place to say the spell and headed over. As he made his way to the cabana, he stuck to the shadows to avoid being seen. He then hid inside while no one was looking, pulled out the spell from his pocket, and read it out in a loud whisper.

"Goddess of the moon and all that is bright, I ask you to unbind me from the unloving one's bite. A bond is meant to be shared in a consented fashion because love should contain passion. Please release me from her domineering alpha ways, so I may love my destined mate in upcoming days."

He had just finished with the spell when he saw the cover of the cabana pull up. He shoved the piece of paper in his pocket before the person behind the white and light blue striped canvas fabric stepped in. Once the light hit the person, he recognized it was Harper.

"Harper! What are you doing here?"

"Oh! I didn't realize they rent these out. You must be getting it ready for someone. I'm sorry! I just wanted to come in here to think."

"Are you okay? I mean, I expected you to be here earlier for that drink."

Her lips thinned as the word drink was uttered.

"Colton, I guess, uh, I should apologize? I—I thought you were dating Blake, and I wanted to avoid all the drama. I'm here for a vacation. Ya get what I mean?"

Colton inched closer to her and palmed her shoulders.

"I can promise you I'm not seeing her. I went on a few dates, and then I broke things off with her." He shrugged his shoulders before continuing, "She did something that was a deal-breaker for me. When she was all over me this afternoon, and then I couldn't find you tonight, I assumed I lost my chance with you because of her jealous streak."

Harper smiled.

"One of your friends set me straight. Raffe, I think his name was? Anyway, we were talking most of the evening about you. I'd come down here around 10 and couldn't find you. Good thing Raffe found me, too. The guys here are pushy. I kept telling them I was waiting for someone, and they had a hard time taking the hint that I didn't want to be bothered."

"I'm sorry. I should have been there." He said while shaking his head slightly. "But at least Raffe was there to help you." He flashed a half-smile at her.

"I—I just wanted to come in here and clear my head before I tried to find you again, but here you are." She licked her lips and swallowed hard. "Listen, about earlier," her voice trailed.

"Yeah, I guess you could say that I needed to think about what happened earlier, too. That's why I'm in here." He closed the distance between the two of them and wrapped an arm around her waist.

She took in a jagged breath, a clear sign she was aroused by his touch. That rushed blood right to his dick, making him want the length of her body pressed to his. Everything muscle below his waist was on fire. His wolf howled within him as his hips ground into hers instinctually. She seemed to fit perfectly in his arms, something he had never thought about before when he was with a woman. Her hand slid up from his waist and palmed his chest. And he could swear his mind went blank about everything but her and what would please her the moment her hand glided over his body.

His wolf let out another howl as his lips found hers. And her response to him seemed to be met with the same neediness as his own. She tasted so good. Sparks of electric current filled his scalp as her hands coiled around the back of his head and played with his thick hair. The sensation of her nails was making his dick strain against the zipper of his Dockers. He was finding it hard to concentrate, but his body seemed to go on autopilot as he palmed her backside to pull her closer to him. He guided her to the only sofa lounge in the cabana. Once her calves touched the seat, he immediately pulled her onto the sofa and straddled her hips.

"I can't stop thinking about you after that first kiss. I want you, Colton."

Her hands fumbled with the buttons on her shirt as she removed it and tossed it to the side. She stopped kissing Colton for a moment, his lips instantly aching at the absence of her mouth. But he rejoiced as she took his hands and placed them on her chest. Heat rushed to his fingertips as he circled her nipples with his thumbs until they became peaked behind the thin fabric of her bra. He slid off the thin straps of her bra, undoing the back hook and tossing it next to her shirt. His mouth hovered over each nipple before he gave them the attention she sought, and he graciously obliged her moans by kissing each one. She shimmied out of her skirt and panties in response to his kisses.

Her pure nakedness compelled him to pull her up into his arms. He would have loved for her to be on top of him, but for the first time in his life, he wanted to please a woman's needs rather than be pleasured himself. He trailed kisses down the length of her body before settling his tongue over her slick folds.

"God, baby, you're beautiful." He said as he sucked her clit. Her hips arched towards his skillful tongue in response.

A wave of pleasure washed over him as he watched her face contort into sheer arousal. Her lips made a beautiful-looking O, making him fantasize how great they'd feel sucking on his cock. He plunged a couple of fingers inside her, and the liquid heat of her sex clamped down around his fingers. As she thrust her waist into his fingers and dug her nails into his shoulders, all he could think about was making her come half a dozen times. An 'oh' and 'ah' escaped her lips intermittently as he continued to make love to her with his mouth, tongue, and fingers. A rush of vanilla hit his tongue, a signal that she was becoming undone beneath him.

"That's it, baby. Come for me." He said in a guttural growl over her center.

"Not that I want to spoil the mood because you were beyond wonderful, but we should probably go get that drink. The girls are probably wondering where I am." She said as she reached for her clothes on the floor.

"I was kinda hoping to make you come a few more times before we had to leave, but yeah, I don't want the girls worrying about you." He smiled and kissed the top of her head. She got dressed, and then he led her out of the cabana.

"What would you like to drink?" She asked him as they walked up to the bar.

"A glass of cab is good."

"That's what I was thinking of having, too." She smiled and then bit her lip. "Listen, if you can't already tell, I like you, Colton. A lot."

She looked like she was about to say something more but swallowed the words.

"I like you a lot, too, Harper. So much so that I can't seem to keep my hands off of you." He placed his hand over hers. "Why don't we take these drinks to go, and then we can head back to that cabana where it's a little less noisy and a lot more private? I think we've got wonderful physical chemistry, but I'd like to get to know you a lot better than that."

"Colton, I really like you. I do, and that's why I also want this to be more than physical."

"I wasn't planning on a one-night-stand or a summer fling—if that is what you are getting at. I promise. I just don't like crowds. That's all." He said as his eyes gazed at the maze of people for Blake before looking back at Harper.

Harper's eyes brightened.

"Yeah, that sounds good, then. I'd like to get to know you better, too."

Harper ordered a bottle of cabernet, and the two reached for their goblets and bottle and started heading over to the cabana. Within a few quick minutes, they were back inside, and Harper inhaled sharply.

"So, normally on a first date kind of thing, I'd ask what you do for a living, but clearly, I already know that," Harper said with a chuckle.

"Yeah, you know what I do for a living, but how about you?"

Harper lowered her gaze.

"Currently, I'm in between jobs."

"Well, that's not really considered a bad thing. I mean, people get laid off all the time. Nothing to be ashamed of! This was the first job I took after my mom passed. In hindsight, it probably wasn't the best decision—but, hey? It's a job—right?" Colton said while patting her on the shoulder, hoping to lift her spirits.

"It's not that. I mean, ugh! I don't know what I mean, I guess."

"Harper, what's wrong?" Colton asked with knitted brows.

"They did not lay me off. My ex fired me, and all because I caught Roger cheating on me." She let out a breath before continuing. "Look, I know we agreed to get to know each other better, but do you mind if we change the subject? I really don't want to talk about my ex. That's a talk for like date two or three. I'd rather talk about things we like."

"Okay, so what music do you like listening to?" He asked it quickly, hoping his wolf would keep quiet.

The hairs on the back of his neck seemed to stand at attention to her pleas to change the subject about her ex. Both he and his wolf didn't like the sound of her voice. Clearly, the ex hurt her, and that wasn't acceptable to Colton. He wanted to protect

Harper from anyone that tried to hurt her. His wolf wanted nothing more than to pummel the asshole for cheating on such a beautiful woman. The ass didn't know how to treat a lady, and Colton was willing to beat the lesson into the guy repeatedly. The only problem with that scenario was that he wasn't sure if he and his wolf could treat Harper any better. He sucked in a breath.

"I like a lot of classic rock."

"So, who is your favorite guitar player of all time, then, Harper?"

This woman, who was methodically thinking about guitar players, clearly deserved a man who could control his temper. And long enough not to want to beat the ex into a bloody pulp. The dickwad shouldn't be more than a footnote in her life. Sure, she didn't want to talk about it, and probably for a bunch of other reasons other than being hurt by him. But damn! Was he going to disappoint her, too?

"I guess I'd have to say Eric Clapton."

"Really? He's like the most over-rated there is."

She laughed.

"Got ya!"

"What do you mean, Harper?"

"I wanted to see if we were on the same page—clearly we are. Eddy Van Halen is really my favorite."

Colton smiled. "Yeah, mine, too."

Harper poured a glass of wine for them both and took a sip from her glass.

"So, what did you do for a living? Can I at least ask that?"

Harper let out a long breath.

"I worked as a paralegal at my last job. Honestly, I should be a lawyer by now." She shrugged her shoulders. "It's not anything I really enjoyed doing. It paid some bills, and that's really about it. The only thing that was nice about it was when Roger and I first started dating." She sighed before continuing. "I was happier back then because at least I felt like I had some kind of purpose. But clearly, he had a different purpose than I had."

"Yeah, I can appreciate that. It's not like I got this job because I've been dreaming about being a cabana boy since kindergarten."

Harper chuckled.

"Yeah, I wouldn't think you would. Guess we both are just trying to get by in life right now. At least it seems that way."

"Well, what is it you really want to do?"

"For a career? I don't know. I really haven't given it much thought beyond helping people with my law degree. There are just so many practices I could get into. Mom and Dad always told me about all of these jobs that I should consider, so I had something to fall back on in case writing—which is my dream job, didn't pan out. Turns out—I enjoy being a lawyer too. So I'll probably look to writing as the dream job after the dream job."

"So you've always wanted to write?"

"Yeah. That and being an editor sounds pretty amazing too. I like helping authors a lot. I've been an ARC reader for so many authors I've lost count. My hundreds of classes of English Comp have proved to many that I'm a valuable ARC reader." She said with a half-smile.

"Well, now that you are between jobs, perhaps you could consider pursuing a writing career?"

"I don't know. Maybe? But I really wouldn't know where to start. Frankly, with my lack of experience, I'd be better off applying for a barista position at the local Starbucks. I really don't see an editing firm picking me up, and writing doesn't always pay bills between gigs, either. At least that's what my folks had always said to me when I was growing up. Given how many authors I know and how little they get paid, I think my parents were right. It's time for me to hunker down and bust my ass for 18 hours a day so I can pay off my college loan. It should only take me another decade and a half to finish paying that off."

"Retail isn't always a great job. I get it—you want to pay off the bills as stress-free as possible. But that kind of job should just be your stepping stone. Especially since your heart is in writing and law. Don't sell yourself short just because you have bills."

Harper took another sip of wine.

"Perhaps you are right. So, what's your dream? What do you want to be once society allows you to grow up?"

"I want to get into construction. It's always been a passion of mine to build things."

"There's something therapeutic about working with your hands."

"Yeah, there is, but I'd rather be on the planning side of it. I'm more into wanting to be an architect."

"What's stopping you?"

Colton shrugged. It was the first time someone had ever asked him this question. Everyone else only asked him questions about his mother and how she was doing.

"My past." He let out a long breath to try to calm himself before she started asking him more questions. He wasn't planning on being *The Crypt*

Keeper with her. The last thing he wanted to be viewed as was a brooding kind of guy, but he wasn't sure if he was ready to tell Harper all about his mother and the cancer that killed her.

"How so?"

"My mother was sick for a very long time, and I dropped out of college early to take care of her. Once she passed, I couldn't bring myself to move on. I've kinda been stuck in limbo, not really knowing what to do with my life. This job turned up, and I thought it was a way to get a tan and get myself focused on living for once."

She put a hand over his.

"I'm sorry to hear that. It sucks losing someone you love. I get it. When my dad died, I wasn't sure about the whole meaning of life thing either. In fact, I never really thought about a sense of purpose until this whole Roger thing came about. Something they never taught you in high school is how to live. They are so focused on showing you how to advance your learning for college. I mean, that's great and all, but our tough decisions in life start the minute we graduate high school. Seems like all the decisions that define us happen in our twenties. After that, we are living and working for the families we are building for our own."

Colton gave her a knowing nod.

"I never really thought about it like that, but you are right. Our twenties are really the only decade that defines the first half of our adult lives."

"Well, yeah. I guess when our children—well—if we choose to have them graduate themselves, we reach another turning point in our lives. But really, by then, we are much older, and our jobs are kind of already mapped out. Guess I'm just used to doing a lot of settling in life because of Roger. I may not know where I see myself in five years, but after searching for what I don't want, I've come to learn more about what I'd like to have in life."

"Well, maybe you can change that for the better now? You're in between jobs, so don't settle this time. Keep looking for something until you wind up with a job you'd enjoy. This way, every time you set foot in your office, you feel good because it won't be just a job to you."

Harper took another sip and smiled.

"You're right. I think I'll take you up on your advice. Are you going to take your own?"

"What do you mean?"

"Well, clearly, Blake isn't letting you pursue your dreams. In fact, that Speedo—"

"Uniform, it's my uniform." He said to her while

crossing his arms. He hated to correct her, but it was the only thing he could do to maintain his dignity at this point. She was right. The damned thing sucked, but he had to keep this job until he found something else.

Harper shook her head.

"Why do you let her treat you this way? You are a person—not an object. If the roles were reversed and I was in a skimpy bathing suit—you'd have words for the boss, right?"

Colton shook his head and shrugged his shoulders.

"Yeah, I would. Women shouldn't be treated as sex symbols, and it never occurred to me that Blake wasn't any different."

"Why? Do you really think you deserve to be treated like this?"

"Look, I understand we are in the 'emotional getting to know you' stage at this point in the conversation, but I think I like things better when we are talking about rock bands." He took a sip of wine before continuing. "When my mom died, I wasn't exactly taking things well. I'm no saint when it comes to dating. Most of my relationships didn't make it past a first date, and all because I didn't want to get hurt. Opening up and telling you about my feelings isn't easy for me."

"None of us are saints, Colton. We all make mistakes. I wasn't saying what I said to make you feel guilty. You don't deserve to be treated like a piece of eye candy—regardless of what happened before." She reassured him by patting him on his hand.

"Yeah, but you probably never slept with someone just to see if you could feel something other than apathy. Harper, I was numb for a very long time—sometimes I wonder if I still am. That's not a normal emotion to have when you are on a first date."

"You seem to be doing quite all right in the feeling department from where I'm standing." She said with a chuckle.

He met her gaze. His lips thinned before he answered her. "I don't know about that."

His wolf was fighting to come to the surface the more time he spent with her. He knew the wolf wanted to claim her, to protect her from all that was going on at this resort. But he wasn't exactly the right person for the job of a protectorate. The immediate threat of Blake was thwarted for the most part tonight, but there was tomorrow and the next day after that. He now understood why Marcus and Raffe stayed behind after finally freeing themselves from Blake. They did it to protect all the innocent humans, unaware of the animalistic dangers they unknowingly cohabitated with at the resort. Harper wasn't safe in this place, and there was no way he could guarantee her safety in his arms, either. Not when he knew the truth about himself, about being a monster.

"It's getting late. Let me walk you back to your room."

"It's not that late!" She said as she pulled out her phone. "It's," The phone's bright light clicked on. "one in the morning. Okay, maybe it is getting late."

She frowned and shoved her phone back into her pocket as the two of them walked into the lobby where the elevator was. Colton pushed the button for the penthouse, and the doors swung open immediately. As they ascended, he watched the numbers go up on the screen above the doors and wondered why they seemed to be moving slower than expected. His wolf growled at him, wanting the forefront of his mind to say goodnight to Harper.

"How about we meet up in that same cabana tomorrow? It can kinda be our little place while you are here." The thought hit his lips before he could stop his wolf from saying it. It was a bad idea to get involved with her, an incredibly awful idea, and he wished his wolf understood that.

She had no idea that he was a monster and that he needed to protect her from himself. The only way to do that was to be clear to her that they couldn't date. But he wouldn't say anything yet. Not until Harper was safely away from Blake and her pack and back home in blissful unawareness of the darkness surrounding her.

"I'd like that very much. But let's make it earlier? I'll make sure to come down from my room before 8 this time." She said with a smile. "Perhaps we can even have a late dinner."

"That would be really nice."

The doors opened as he faced her, smiling. She ducted out of the cart and slowly walked towards her door. Once she was at it, she turned on her heel and laced her fingers around the back of his head.

"I had a really nice time tonight."

Colton smiled.

"I did too."

"Want to come in for a nightcap? Pretty sure the bar is fully stocked."

"I don't want to bother your friends. They are probably sleeping."

"Just one drink? Please? I don't want to end the evening just yet."

He cupped her cheek.

"How can I say no to that face?"

She smiled, opened the door, and led him into the penthouse. The room had a hallway that led to a master bath area that contained a jetted tub. She walked past that area and opened up the heavy royal blue curtains that led to the balcony.

"I must admit, this is a very nice room. I normally don't get this lucky when it comes to someone trying to make up for a mistake." She smiled as she crossed over to the desk that was near the miniature fridge. "I think there is some wine in here somewhere. That's probably the best thing without having to go grab some ice." She grabbed two small bottles of a cabernet from the mini-fridge and then proceeded to pour the red liquid into the glass tumblers that were on the oak desk next to the fridge. As she handed him one of the glasses, she turned to open up the sliding doors that led to the balcony overlooking the ocean. She sat on the outdoor couch, placed her glass on the coffee table, and motioned for Colton to sit next to her. Colton placed his glass next to her and sat down. He looked up at the inky black sky dotted with bright stars and let out a breath he wasn't aware he was holding in. She took a quick sip of her wine and then met his gaze.

"A penny for your thoughts."

He wasn't thinking about anything except how much he'd been enjoying this evening with her. It was the first time since his mother died that he was actually happy. It never occurred to him before that he was holding a lot of himself in. With her, it was easy to do everything, including breathing. Before her, he thought little about his feelings. Opening up to someone was just too hard. But her light conversation lifted his spirits, making conversation so much easier than it'd been in years. This made him realize Harper was far more than just a one-night stand. She was for keeps.

A pang hollowed out his stomach as he came to the realization that he was starting to care for the woman before him, and that was going to make things complicated if he had any hopes of protecting her from his wolf and the pack.

"Hmm?"

"You are looking like you are a million miles away. Are you okay? I'm not boring you already —am I?"

"No, no! I'm just—uh? I guess what I mean to

say is that this is the first time in an extremely long time that I'm enjoying myself. This has been a really awesome date, Harper."

She smiled.

"I'm glad you are enjoying yourself. I'm enjoying myself too." She scooted closer to him and placed her head on his shoulder before looking up at the stars.

"I've lived in northern Texas for a few years now, and I really love the city life in Fort Worth, especially the Sundance Square area, but I never really took the time to look up at the stars. I guess it's because I've got family in New York City and, of course, there really aren't a lot of stars to look at because the city is polluted with neon lights and street lamps. This is really nice. Very peaceful."

"You've never gone star-gazing, I take it?"

"Nope. Never had the chance. I mean, I have an app on my phone, but I've never been able to use it."

Colton smiled and pointed his index finger out past her head towards the sky.

"Well, right there—the four stars that make a big box—that's the big dipper."

"Okay, so I'm guessing over there," she pointed to the right of the large dotted box in the sky before continuing, "is the little dipper—right?"

"Yup, you'd be right."

"I take it you are more from the country part of Texas?"

"Yeah. My backyard was my parents' farm. When I was little, Dad and I would pitch a tent near the family firepit, and he'd point out all the constellations. I've forgotten most of them now that I'm older, but it was still a really nice memory to have before he passed away.

"It sure sounds like it. I never did anything cool like that in our backyard. But my mom taught me how to bake a cake." She chuckled a little before continuing. "I was so excited because I thought she was going to teach me how to bake it from scratch. My grandma taught me how to make homemade pasta, so I figured my mom was going to teach me the same way. On the day we were going to bake, she put a Duncan Hines cake box in front of me and told me to read the directions. It was not the most fun experience with my mom while growing up, but it's a memory." She said as she shrugged her shoulders. "I loved my mother for many reasons. She was strong. She had a huge passion for teaching little kids. But she wasn't the best cook."

"Sounds like she was an exceptional woman despite her lack of skills in the kitchen, though."

Harper reached for the glass on the coffee table and brought the red liquid towards her lips.

"She most certainly was a remarkable woman. I wish I were more like her. She had no fear of anything. I've never met anyone quite like that in my life. I'm basically scared of everything." She said as she crossed her arms. "If I were a bit braver in life, I probably never would have fallen for Roger. You have your ex, Blake—I have mine. And frankly, I think your ex is nicer than mine."

"How so?" He asked as he rubbed her shoulders when she began to shudder.

"It was really nice in the beginning. I thought I had found my soulmate. We were even engaged. But once that ring was on my finger, he changed. It was almost as if I was more like a piece of property rather than the love of his life. And then he cheated on me. I broke things off, of course, but as retaliation, he fired me. So now I'm between jobs." She said with a sigh. "Hopefully, someone will hire me when I get back. He's pretty prominent, so he may have blackballed me from a few of the neighboring law firms."

Colton tucked a few loose strands of hair behind her ear.

"I'm sorry that happened to you, but frankly, I'm

glad he let you go because then it gave us a chance to meet." He said while licking his lips.

"I guess when you look at it that way, you are right. I would never have come here if things were good between Roger and me. Frankly, I almost didn't, but my friends convinced me otherwise, and I'm delighted they did. I'm really enjoying spending time with you."

He inched closer to her and cupped her cheek.

"I will definitely second that. You are a special person, Harper. I've never met anyone quite like you."

He slipped an arm around her waist and closed the distance between the two of them. His lips pressed against hers with a sense of urgency. Her hands wrapped around his neck as her chest pressed into his.

"You really are amazing." He breathed over her lips as his chest rumbled out a low growl.

"I want you, Colton."

Her lips grazed over his jawline before she kissed his neck. His inner wolf was howling at the thought of claiming her as his very own, but he was worried that if he didn't make it back to his room at a somewhat reasonable hour, Blake would come looking for him. The woman was always seeking him out, and she was quite the stalker when it came to him. The thing was, he didn't want to leave her yet. Tomorrow was Saturday, and he had a mid-shift, so convincing himself to stay another hour with Harper in his arms wasn't all that hard to do.

"I want you, too."

CHAPTER 8

WHO LET THE DOG OUT?

Harper led him into the bedroom before closing the door. Colton pressed his front to her back, moved her locks away from her neck, and pressed hot, wet kisses from her chin to her collarbone. She was the most beautiful girl he'd ever met, and an hour wasn't enough for him to show her just how much he wanted to please her. But he would not waste even a minute with her, so he turned her around to face him and scooped her into his arms, and placed her gently on the bed before he removed his clothing and hers.

Before he threw his Dockers on the floor, he pulled out a condom he tucked in his right front pocket and slid it over his dick, which was already twitching to be inside of her.

"God, Harper! You are so damned beautiful."

He couldn't keep his hands off of her, wanting to explore every inch of her body, paying attention to all of her soft moans and committing to memory every swirl of his tongue, lips, and thrust that pleased her. Her body wasn't just something he had to study, no. He wanted to worship her every single night. And something told him he'd never stop unless she sent him away.

The sun peeked out of the window shade. The early light warmed his skin. He smiled, his eyes still closed and sleepy as thoughts of Harper in his arms flooded his still foggy head. The dreams he was still having of her seemed so vivid that it was almost as if he could still feel her in his arms.

An alarm rang out in the room, and he quickly opened his eyes to find unfamiliar surroundings.

Shit! I fell asleep in her suite! I've got to get back to my place before Blake discovers I've been out all night!

He shut off the alarm that was on his watch and slipped his arm out from underneath her neck. Quickly, he pulled on his clothes and snuck out the door. He was already halfway to his own room when Colton realized he should have left her a note saying how much he enjoyed spending time with her. If he had the time after taking his shower, he was going to have half a dozen long-stemmed red roses sent up to her room. That should suffice for his blunder and show her he really enjoyed the evening.

He was about to hold his keycard up to the door when Blake came off of the elevator.

Shit!

"Why aren't you in uniform yet, and why are you wearing the same outfit you did last night?"

"I went out for an early morning walk. Figured with that poor excuse for a uniform, I should start working a little more cardio into my routine. The walk did me good, and I think by next week, I'll take up jogging on the beach."

He held his breath in as she peered at him, clearly searching his eyes, trying to catch him in the blatant lie he had just conjured. He was so grateful to the brothers for giving him that hematite necklace because he hoped that would be enough to keep her from concluding that he was lying right to her face.

"You outright disobeyed my orders! How could you do that after everything I've given you?" She said as she crossed her arms. "I should have you confined to your room for such insubordinate behavior."

"What are you talking about, Blake?"

"You slept with her! I know the walk of shame when I see it! I told you nothing can get past me."

"I did no such thing."

He tried to look as convincing as possible, but he knew it would take a lot to keep up the lie.

"Well, I will not confine you because I think we can come to an understanding. After all, we are in a relationship, and I'm not completely unforgiving. Therefore, if you stay away from the home wrecker, I won't have to kill her. Is that understood?"

"Blake, what are you talking about? We are not in a relationship. And you can't be serious about killing her!"

"I can smell the slut all over you! How can you just stand there and lie right to my face? You are my mate, and I made you mine when I claimed you. If you so much as even look at that bitch, I will kill her before you take your next breath. Do I make myself clear?"

The fire building up in her eyes was enough to convince him that Blake was serious. And no matter how much he loathed Blake, he had no choice but to obey her for Harper's protection. Blake and her pack were dangerous, and the last thing Colton wanted was for Harper, and her friends, to become slaves to Blake's pack. He had to agree with Blake to keep everyone safe, and hopefully, Harper would one day forgive him for what he was about to do.

Harper looked at her watch for what seemed like the hundredth time in the past 45 minutes. He was late, and she couldn't help but wonder if he was standing her up. He had profusely said that he wasn't into Blake, but that didn't stop Harper from thinking that he may very well be with the woman.

The bartender placed a glass of wine in front of her.

"Oh, no—there must be some sort of mistake. I didn't order this." She said as she pushed the glass towards the bartender.

"It's from Colton." The cute blonde bartender said with a smile. "He can't come over but wanted to make sure you had this as an apology." She smiled again before bouncing over to the other side of the bar.

Harper slid the glass back towards her and took a sip. It was only then that she noticed Colton at the other end of the bar and with Blake, who was hanging all over him yet again. His eyes locked onto hers as Blake pulled him into her arms and kissed his neck.

Oh, hell no! This isn't happening!

Harper got up from where she was sitting and headed over to Colton and Blake. There was no way in hell she was going to lose to this bitch. Colton may not want her, but she didn't care. That bitch had the nerve to shove her tongue down his throat. Harper could see he was squirming out of Blake's grip, and Harper would not let a woman molest a guy who didn't want her advances. Colton's eyes widened with each one of her steps toward him and Blake. She wasn't sure if the fear that flashed in his eyes was getting caught or what, but she continued to walk toward the clearly unhappy couple.

He seemed nervous, and Harper took that as a clue that he'd, in fact, been lying to her this whole time. There must be at least something between the two of them for him to be around Blake. After last night, though, she'd hoped Colton would be with her instead of Blake the bitch. Harper hated the fact that she was naïve. Colton looked at her as a one-night stand. He just wanted to get in her pants—that seemed abundantly clear at this point. And even though Colton's back was now facing her, he had to be enjoying the makeup session from Blake—right? Harper's neck came on fire as she watched Blake's palms cupping Colton's ass cheeks and kissing him as if they were they were the only people in the room. The sight alone made Harper's stomach twist and turn with bile, but she couldn't let Blake see her disgust. Not now, not ever. This time, she was going to grow a pair and confront the bitch head-on.

"Colton! Thanks for the drink." She smiled brightly as she approached. There were only mere inches between them, and Blake's eyes grew fixated on hers.

"That wasn't from Colton, darling. That was from me. I felt bad that you were in the bar's corner all by your lonesome. You should be out on the dance floor enjoying yourself and staying as far away from my Colton as possible."

Colton frowned and continued to squirm out of Blake's grip, but she latched onto his hips tighter.

"Are you really that batshit of a bitch? Or are you

not 'Hooked on Phonics'? The man isn't into you, Blake."

"We are dating, so again, stay away from him." Blake as she slinked an arm around Colton's shoulders and draped her hand over his chest.

Colton removed her arm from around his shoulders immediately.

"Doesn't look like Colton agrees with the assessment of your delusion."

Harper smirked and winked at the woman. She then slung the rest of the wine in her glass all over Blake's lap.

"You little bitch!"

Blake's voice was a low growl that formed deep within her chest. She stood up with her hand cocked and slapped Harper across the face.

"I'm sorry, it was an accident. The people on the dance floor bumped into me, causing my arm to jerk." Harper said while she rubbed the side of her cheek. "And hasn't anyone ever taught you? That's no way to be treating a paying customer, Blake? First, you are threatening me, then you call me names, and now you assault me? I'll be sure to leave a scathing review on Yelp."

"You poured your drink all over me! How is that not assault?"

"I am a lawyer, Blake. You don't want to fuck with me. What I did was criminal mischief at best. And I can have that charge thrown out, stating evidence of what's been spewing out of your mouth this past weekend. You are an abusive and delusional twat!" Her face reddened with each word she spat into Blake's face.

Colton put himself between her and Blake and lengthened the distance by gently pushing on each woman's shoulder.

"Okay, Blake, I think it's time for you to go and get changed." He said to her as his eyes locked onto hers. A chill bit through the air as many of the customers stopped talking to stare at the three of them.

"Wait! You are taking her side?" She shrieked as she crossed her arms.

"I'm not taking either side here. Not when this is a pissing match, and neither of you has the balls to make it go the distance. Now get back to your room and take a shower to cool off, Blake."

"But?"

"But nothing! You were more out of line than normal. Go cool off before the rest of the guests see you making a scene. It's bad enough that I have to fan off the flames with the group near us. This is going to cost you a round of free drinks, and you know it!"

Blake pouted and then let out a long breath.

"You are right. I've let my temper get the best of me. Do what you need to for damage control. We can't afford any bad press right now. Not with the pandemic the way it is." Blake said in a low voice as she scanned the surrounding crowd. She let out a long breath and scampered off towards the front entrance of the hotel.

Colton watched her until she entered and then turned his gaze to Harper. His lips down-turned slightly, and Harper lowered her gaze from him.

"Okay, okay, I'll admit that I wasn't acting very mature with her. And I'm sorry if I made you uncomfortable. It's just that she's making me crazy! I hate the way she treats you!"

Colton placed his hands on her shoulders.

"Hey, why don't you let me worry about that, okay? In the meantime, will you please sit here at the bar while I do damage control? I'll get you a drink along with the rest of this crowd that saw Blake's tantrum. When I'm done—I'd like to talk."

Harper smiled while shaking her head.

"I like that. You know, you really are too good to

Blake. Most employees would just let her sink. You are more of a manager than she will ever be."

Colton smiled. It was the first time someone outside of his family had ever paid him a compliment about his work ethic, and that made his heart squeeze.

CHAPTER 9

FOR THE LOVE OF DOGS

Blake entered her room and headed straight for the fridge to grab the bottle of chard she always had on hand for emergencies. She never let a bitch from the resort get to her before. Until now, she felt confident about getting any man she liked. But Harper seemed to prove to be the thorn that Blake never thought existed. She grabbed a goblet and an opener from her bar stand and then headed to her master bathroom, where she peeled off her wine-stained jeans.

She was glad the wine she ordered Harper was a chardonnay. It was easier to get the stains out as opposed to a red, but it still shouldn't have happened. Every day that Harper was staying at the hotel was another day she was losing her connection with Colton. She understood the risks when she bit him. He might reject her, but he knew nothing about pack rules, and she was confident her alpha strength would get him to submit. She didn't want to lie to him because he had an out. He didn't have to remain her mate, but she wanted some time to plead her case with him. Colton was gorgeous, and merely being around him made her panties drenched. Her wolf wanted to make pups in the worst way. And that's why she had to fight for Colton. Clearly, she now had to up her game, and she planned on doing that by taking Harper out of the equation.

Colton can't yearn for someone who isn't among the living. He'll learn to love me once I get rid of her.

Blake smiled into her full-length mirror and splashed some water on her face before stepping into the steaming shower. Water beaded on her skin as she lathered over all the sticky wine that still clung to her body.

"I'm really sorry. I was acting like I was a jealous, lovesick teenager."

"Forget about it."

"It's just Blake makes me nuts. I don't know what it is about her, but I really can't stand her. I know it has to do with hating how she treats you. That I won't apologize for. Nor will I apologize for standing my ground with her. It wasn't until I got up to the both of you at the bar that I realized she was trying to get me to concede in whatever stupid game she's convinced we are playing. And I can't do that with her or with you. I really care about you, and I think you are worth fighting for because you deserve to be with someone that cares about you. But, having said all of that, I am truly sorry if I made things weird between us."

Colton smiled and tucked a strand of hair behind Harper's ear.

"If I'm being honest, it was kinda cute how you were sticking up for me." He placed his palms on her shoulders. "I'm all set with damage control. Want to head over to the cabana? I owe you a drink, and since the owner fucked up royally today, she won't know if she's missing a bottle. Red or white?"

"White," Harper said with a smile.

He reached over the bar to grab two goblets, and the bartender passed him a bottle of Fetzer, her favorite chardonnay. He then draped an arm around Harper and led her to the cabana they were in last night. After pouring them both a glass, he handed one over to Harper.

"I shouldn't say this because I shouldn't condone it, but you dumping your drink all over Blake was awesome. The look on her face was priceless."

Harper giggled.

"I'm glad you aren't horribly upset with me. I must admit that I didn't want to be so immature about the situation. Still, Blake has that certain personality where she gets to you. It's strange to admit this, but I have had no one get under my skin like that since, well, since high school."

"Yeah, Blake is kinda like that with me, too. I really want nothing to do with her anymore. Not since—" Colton's voice trailed as he swallowed hard.

Colton knew he shouldn't tell Harper what he was because he'd risk not only exposing himself but the brothers in the pack that he cared about, too. As for the rest of the pack? He honestly didn't care. Blake sealed their fate the minute she allowed herself to turn innocent norms into werewolves.

Harper put a hand over his palm.

"Colton, it's okay. You can tell me anything. I hope you get that."

"I do. It's just—"

The sound of cloth ripping broke Colton's thoughts. Sharp claws became visible as they broke through the cabana cloth. Harper's eyes widened as what appeared to be a large, dark grey dog leaped into the enclosed area.

"Oh my God! It's a timber wolf!"

Colton turned to Harper and reached for her hand.

"Harper, that's no ordinary wolf." He said to her as he placed her body behind his.

Harper's eyes narrowed as she tried to process what Colton was saying to her.

"What are you talking about, Colton?"

"I didn't want you finding out this way. I was going to tell you, and then she came in here. Do you trust me?" He asked, squeezing her hand while never taking his eyes off of the wolf that was growling and dripping saliva from its mouth.

"Yes."

"Good."

He squeezed her hand again and then got on all fours as his body twisted and contorted in flashes before Harper's eyes. Muscles in his back grew to inhuman proportions. His hair changed to white fur, and his hands and feet transformed into paws.

Harper gasped in disbelief.

"Colton? You're a? You, you're a wolf?"

The white wolf before her whimpered as the other dark grey wolf in the cabana bit down on his hind leg. The white wolf turned to the grey wolf and growled. Vibration from the white wolf's growl shook the entire cabana. Harper let out a shaky breath as Colton then raised his front paw and swiped at the grey wolf's abdomen. The grey wolf whimpered and skulked into a darker corner of the cabana behind one of the royal blue and white striped couches. After a few moments, Blake's head emerged from behind the couch. Harper gasped.

"You're a wolf, too?"

"Yes, I am, Harper, and that makes me a better mate for Colton! How could you—a mere mortal ever date a shifter? Face it, you're both from different worlds, and you would never understand Colton's wolf!"

Colton immediately shifted back to his human form.

"That's enough, Blake! It's over. I don't want you as my mate. Not now, not ever! I think I've been perfectly clear about that from the beginning. But since you can't take a hint, I will make this abundantly clear. I denounce you as my mate and my alpha. No one has a claim to me. I am my own being."

A white mist filled the air, and then electric energy filled the room. It was as if Colton's words charged the energy around them all. He reached for Harper's hand. "Let's get out of here."

Harper pulled her hand away from Colton's.

"Oh, I'm getting out of here, all right, but not with you!" She said before running past them both.

She ran all the way to the elevators without looking back.

How could he have kept such a thing from me? And then ask me to trust him? How can I trust him after he shifted into a werewolf? For Christ's sake, wolves aren't exactly domesticated.

She let out a breath she'd been holding in since the cabana.

Two days. Two more stinking days at this place! I can't exactly tell the girls why I want to leave, and I can't show my face downstairs for fear of running into Colton and Blake. Maybe I should just go on my own?

The opening of the doors from the elevator cart broke her train of thought. She ducked out and bounced into the penthouse.

I can always order room service. This way, I wouldn't have to run into either of them.

She plopped herself on her bed, face down, and allowed the tears to flow. In all of her years of dating, she'd never been hurt this deeply. Sure, Roger was a jerk, and it hurt that all he wanted was arm candy. But even when Roger was at his worst, Harper knew she could do better than him. She thought Colton was precisely that, better. But even he had an affliction of not telling the whole truth. Before she had known it, sleep overcame her from her exhaustion from encountering the werewolves.

The morning sun peeked through the one part of the curtain that Harper couldn't get to close. And even though the bright light warmed her skin, her heart felt as if she was in the artic. She let out a sigh and dragged herself to the kitchen in the living area of their suite so she could make coffee.

The sun was still a purple, orange hue in the sky,

signifying it was still very early in the morning. Silence filled the entire penthouse suite at this hour of the morning, and Harper almost wanted to cry again so she could use up all of her tears before her friends woke and began asking questions. But even though she wasn't looking forward to the barrage of questions, she still wanted her friends around her. Rallying her and telling her that Colton was an asshat for lying. She understood him keeping something so huge from her. But he should have said something before they'd gotten so intimate. Still, she wouldn't blab his secret. Not in a million years. She may hate Colton for lying to her, but him being a werewolf wasn't exactly a secret for her to spill to her friends. Deep down, she knew she had to keep this secret for Colton's sake.

What if I take a walk on the beach? That could take up most of the morning and kill enough time. So that I don't feel so alone with my stupid thoughts.

She let out a sigh.

Who the fuck am I kidding? I can't tell anyone about what happened last night because they will all think I'm crazy! Shit! It's not like I can tell anyone about the real me either, and for the same damned reason!

She poured some creamer and sugar into her coffee and took a sip. Once she was done, she washed out the cup and then pulled on some biker shorts and a tee shirt so she could take a walk on the beach.

As she took a few steps towards the water's edge, she noticed a familiar figure jogging down the beach.

Crap! I didn't want to run into him at all! I figured being out this early was a safe bet!

"Harper! Wait up?" She heard Colton say, and she froze at the words.

"Colton, I'm sure you want to get your run in before your shift begins. So I won't keep you."

Her words came out as cold as she was feeling. She didn't mean to sound like such a bitch, especially with a guy whose last relationship was with a batshit crazy and possessive werewolf.

"I just want to see how you are doing. Please? Tell me you are doing somewhat okay."

Harper crossed her arms.

"I'm not sure how to answer that. I mean, it's not every day you see a man turn into an enormous wolf."

"Yeah, I get it. It's a little mind-blowing, I'm sure. But I'm also sure you can understand that I'd appreciate it if you kept my secret. We shifters hide our wolf's side from normal humans because there's less potential for exposure that way."

"I wouldn't ever tell anyone, Colton! I hoped you'd know that about me by now. And honestly, even if I wanted to, I doubt anyone would believe me. Plus, I get it. I mean—I'm still mad at you. Don't get me wrong! But I, too, have a secret to keep so I can protect my family. And maybe I should have told you about it, but that doesn't exactly matter now--does it?"

Thoughts of what Blake had said to her last night rang through Harper's ears.

"Yes, I am, Harper, and that makes me a better mate for Colton! How could you—a mere mortal ever date a shifter? Face it, you're both from different worlds, and you would never understand Colton's wolf!"

She shook her head, hoping her brain could focus on the words she wanted to say to him as he was giving her--dare she say it? Puppy dog eyes. But the look in his eyes quickly diminished.

"Yeah, I guess that would make sense. I'm just really sorry you had to find out that way. And I'm sure you have questions, especially now that I'm no longer part of the pack."

"Colton, I'm still in too much shock to be thinking about questions. Besides, what's there to ask? I mean, let's face it, Blake was right. We pretty much come from two different worlds."

She let out a long breath, wanting him to give her some time to tell him that she was a witch. And not the Wicca kind that the tree huggers talk about. Nope. She had powers, real ones that could move mountains or bend any other element if she wanted to.

Colton's jaw tightened as she opened her mouth, readying herself to tell him her truth. She didn't want to hide it from him, but she thought he was an ordinary guy and would freak out if he found out what she could do. Part of her wanted to blurt it out because she felt guilty for being mad at him for keeping his secret. Still? Hers wasn't as dangerous-- at least as far as she was concerned. Sure, her spells could do damage to not only the elements around her but even to the human mind if she practiced the dark arts. But she'd never do that! She was as white a witch as they came because she only used her magic against evil beings that'd harm humans. Beings like vampires and rogue shifters who cared little for human life.

"Yeah, I guess you are right. Well, listen, I don't want to keep you from your walk. I've got to head back to my room to get ready for my shift, anyway."

Harper opened her mouth to respond, but Colton turned on his heel and ran in the opposite direction towards the resort complex. Harper blew out another breath she didn't realize she was holding as she watched him run all the way back to the entrance of the hotel. Harper really wanted to tell him what she was, but if she did, she'd run the risk of hurting him more than Harper already had.

The idea of him lying felt less and less like the reason why she wanted to put distance between the two of them and more and more like an excuse.

Guess it's just as well that I pissed him off. It's not like we could work. He's a shifter, and I'm a witch. It would never, ever work. He'd never love me if he knew I killed some of his kind that hurt humans.

CHAPTER 10

DOGGIE HEAVEN

It had been 6 months since her trip to Pearl South Padre Island Resort & Spa beach resort and 6 long months since she last saw Colton run away from her on the beach. She had tried to put him out of her mind. But Harper found it extremely difficult to forget the man that made her feel more like a whole person rather than the shell of a person she'd been living like. For too long, she was numb, especially after she'd broken it off with Roger.

She'd been lying awake at night thinking about Colton and how much she truly cared for him. The more time she spent in the world of normal humans, the more she realized she'd rather be in his world of shifters. The thing that kept her up the most was her not giving Colton a chance. She shouldn't have been so mad at him for keeping his secret because she had one, too. Humans—except for Zoey and Chloe—didn't get her witchy side. She rarely trusted anyone enough to tell them. She didn't even tell Roger, and she was engaged to him. Harper was always so grateful that the two most important people in her life kept her secret. And when Colton trusted her with his secret about being a shifter, the first chance she got, she ran. And it was all out of fear of getting hurt again—not because he was a werewolf. Harper understood that now.

The argument they had was stupid and still hung over Harper. Sadly, it most likely drove Colton into Blake's arms, and Harper wouldn't blame him if he were married to Blake by this point. She hated to admit it, but Blake was right. She was a better mate for Colton because they were both shifters.

A chill overcame her spine, and she rubbed her arms to stimulate a sense of warmth. But she hadn't had that since she was in Colton's arms. Every effort on her part to comfort herself these past months wasn't working. She walked over to the thermostat in her office to raise the tempera-ture, but even that didn't seem to warm the chill over her body, either. Despite Roger's desperate attempts to blackball her from the legal community, she'd been able to find a new job as a lawyer with a highly established firm called Goldstein & Berliner. She even made a new friend at the firm, Layla Gallo, who'd made partner just before Harper had come on board. The firm handled many famous cases in the normal world, but it also had clients and lawyers that were witches and shifters.

The work was satisfying and also a great distraction from how awful she felt about how she had left things with Colton. What she was doing was making a difference in the world, and that also helped ease some of the pain. But no matter how many depositions she'd pour over for her cases, Colton continued to haunt her mind.

"Knock, knock!" Said Zoey as she peeked her head through the door. "You ready for lunch?"

"Zoey!" Harper said with a sigh while glancing at her calendar. "I forgot we scheduled a lunch."

"Oh, no, you don't, Harper. You are not canceling on me again this week! I haven't seen you in ages. We've barely talked since that vacation, and now that Valentine's Day is coming up tomorrow, I want us to keep as busy as possible. We single people need to stick together. Especially now, since Chloe has got a boyfriend."

"Fine, we will go out to lunch, but I hope you don't mind—it's going to be a working lunch."

"I know you need something to keep your mind off of Colton, but, girl, that's why I'm here. Let's have some time to enjoy each other's company."

Harper ran her fingers through her hair.

"No matter how I try to keep myself occupied, I just can't. I really fucked up with Colton."

"Chin up, Harper. Things will get better. Perhaps we should go to the bar tonight and sing a little karaoke because that always cheers you up." Zoey said as she put a palm on one of Harper's shoulders.

"Maybe you are right. A little fun probably is in order. Lord knows staying home and staring at the ceiling tiles while trying to fall asleep isn't working."

"Then it's settled! We are getting our groove on tonight!"

Harper took one last look in the mirror before heading out to Rusty's for a night of karaoke with Zoey. Not that she really needed to look her best because she didn't plan on putting herself out there. After fucking up with Colton, the last thing she wanted to do was get back on the horse again. It had taken her a long time to get over Roger, but with Colton, everything was different. Nothing seemed settled.

Once Harper got to the bar, she found Zoey in the corner—their usual spot. And she was sitting next to a familiar male figure with dark locks. His black tee clung to his chest in all the right places, signifying a glorious eight-pack.

No! It can't be—can it?

As she inched closer, the familiar muscular frame became more apparent.

"Colton? Is that you?"

"Hi, Harper."

Her eyes darted from Colton's to Zoey's.

"You set me up—didn't you?"

"Harper, it's not like that! I swear! I did not know that Colton would be here! He came in five minutes before you showed up."

"Please don't blame Zoey. It's true. I had no idea I'd run into either of you. I just moved to the area and thought I'd stop in with Marcus and Raffe."

Harper frowned.

"Oh, so you are still with Blake, I take it? How is that going?"

Colton got up from his seat and palmed Harper's shoulders.

"Harper, I was never with Blake—you know that. In fact, the minute you checked out of the hotel was the minute I quit the resort. Well, after I denounced myself from Blake's pack and being her mate, I left. I work as a mechanic at the garage just up the road from here, and I also work construction."

"Oh? That's cool. I guess you are a man of many talents, then."

"You could say that. I do mechanic work as a side gig. I'm mostly into construction. November to March is kinda slow, so I help my Uncle John during the downtime. How about you? What is keeping you busy these days? I know you were between jobs when we talked about it at the resort."

"I work for the Goldstein and Berliner firm. Believe it or not, they actually have a lion shifter as a client, and the girl I work with, Layla Gallo, is a witch. Hopefully, in a couple of years, I can make partner." Harper said with a half-smile.

"Well, that's awesome! I'm happy for you!"

"Hey, Harper, I'll be back. I just saw Chloe walk in, and she didn't see me flag her down."

"Raffe and Marcus spotted her and are directing

her over here. Maybe we can all hang out together?" Colton said.

Harper let out a nervous laugh.

"Actually, I want to get my groove on. Do Marcus and Raffe like to dance?" Asked Zoey.

"We absolutely love to dance but only on one condition." Said Marcus with a wink before continuing. "Dance with both of us."

Zoey smiled and led them both onto the dancefloor. Chloe headed to the bar where her boyfriend Miles tended the bar.

"I guess they all figured we needed some time alone."

Harper began playing with the cocktail napkin in front of her because it was the only thing in sight that she could use to hide her shaking hands.

"Harper, listen. The past six months have been hell for me. I hate the way we left things between us. Running away from you and not giving you a chance to explain was a dick move. I was an ass who should have given you time to process things. I'm sorry, and I hope you can forgive me."

"I didn't exactly give you a chance to explain yourself, either. I was in shock and also hurt that you didn't trust me with your secret. And for that, I'm really sorry, myself. I mean, it's not an everyday conversation to bring up to someone you barely know that you're a shifter. Just like it's not every day you bring up in conversation that you're a powerful witch." Harper bit her lip.

"Of course, this all makes more sense now. I mean, normals rarely fall for shifters—they somehow innately know to stay away from us. And because you are a witch, well, that must have been why it was so easy for me to be around you and control my wolfy side. Witches can resonate with a shifter's vibrational aura. Must be why I always felt so calm and more like myself with you when we were at the resort."

"These past six months have been hell for me, too. I've missed you something awful, and I want no more secrets between us. Can you forgive me for not telling you I'm a witch?" Harper patted the top of Colton's hand and gave him a half-smile.

Colton smiled back at her and tucked a stray hair behind her ear.

"Of course! I want nothing more than to start over with you. Can I buy you a drink and possibly talk you into doing some terrible karaoke duet singing?"

Colton lifted Harper's hand, the one that was still cradling his, and pressed a soft kiss to her knuckles. Harper's breath hitched as an electric heat rushed through her body. A familiar warmth that she welcomed. She missed the strong connection she'd had with him for so long, and now he was back here with her. All seemed right in the world.

"Wait, did you feel that? There's this charged heat between us every time you touch me."

"Yes. That connection has always been there between us, and it's there because you're my fated mate."

"This may sound crazy, but I already knew that. Sometimes being psychic has its perks. I'd definitely like that drink, Colton, but I'm not so sure about the karaoke. Will you settle for some dancing?"

"As long as I get to grind my hips against that gorgeous body of yours, I'll be content. What would you like? Cab?"

"Yes, please."

He ordered a glass for each of them and raised his goblet to hers.

"Here's to new beginnings."

"To new beginnings," Harper said as the glasses made a clinking sound. She took a sip and carefully placed the glass on the cocktail napkin. "So remember when you asked if I had questions while we were on the beach? Well, I do."

Colton swallowed and placed the glass on the bar top.

"Shoot."

"Does it hurt? When you shift, I mean."

Colton shook his head.

"No. It's just a tingling sensation, mostly. Seeing myself transform for the first time kind of was freaky, though."

"Do you get to control when it happens? Or are the myths about werewolves for real where you bark at the full moon?"

Colton chuckled.

"No, we can control when we shift. In the beginning, I thought the same as you because Blake said I needed her to keep me from losing control. But it's easier to keep my wolf at bay now that I'm not around that toxic bitch."

"How is Blake not your alpha? I mean, won't you always have a connection with her?"

Colton took Harper's hand into his again.

"No. The connection is severed. I denounced Blake as my alpha, so now I'm free to be a lone wolf. The only person I answer to is myself. But I did move in with Raffe and Marcus, so I kinda have to listen to them when they as me to do my own dishes." Colton said with a smile. "We sort of formed a lone wolf pack, in a way. Once you checked out, I called for a pack meeting and challenged Blake by breaking the wolf bond connection. She said she that over me since she was the one that bit me. If she had been honest with me from the start, she would have never claimed me to begin with. The wolf bond is sacred, and you enter into it knowing that the coupling is for life. Blake neglected to mention any of that, and she even neglected to mention she was a shifter before she bit me. Turns out the council got wind of her actions, and they disbanded her pack and exiled her to the mountains in Wyoming. Normal humans don't inhabit certain towns around there, so she can't hurt anybody anymore. But to keep her from hurting anyone, an alpha named Donovan is monitoring her movements."

"Well, I'm glad she can't hurt anyone. Blake wasn't the nicest person." Harper said with a half-smile.

An MC's voice came over the loudspeaker, interrupting their conversation.

"It's Valentine's weekend, and you know what that means. Time to hold your honey tight."

A slow tempo blares through the speakers, and Colton squeezes Harper's hand.

"Dance with me?"

"Sure."

Colton whisks Harper off onto the dance floor and then pulls her into his arms. The length of his hard body pressed against hers perfectly. Notes of bergamot and cedar touched her nose as she rested her head on his shoulder. She greedily took in a deep breath to commit his delicious scent to memory.

One dance turned into 5, and within a few short hours, they were talking like they once did during the summer in the cabana. Harper had him follow her back to her place. He parked next to her in the complex, and she led him up to her condo. Her hands were shaking as she fiddled with the keys to unlock her door. Once she opened it and walked through, she plopped her purse on one of the accent chairs, along with draping her coat over the back of it, and then tossed her keys onto the side table next to the chair.

"Would you like a drink? I've got a bottle of red in my wine fridge."

"That sounds great. Want some help to open the bottle?"

"Sure."

She led him to the kitchen, where she opened the cabinet above the wine fridge and grabbed two wine goblets. Then she fished out a bottle opener from one of the nearby drawers. She handed him the opener and the bottle, and he had the bottle open within a minute. The sound of the liquid pouring into the glass filled the room.

"So funny story—I actually just moved into this condo complex myself yesterday."

"Really? Guess I'd better start calling you neighbor then, huh?"

Colton smiled.

"I could get used to that." He said as he pulled her close to him and cupped her cheek. "Ever since I saw you again at the bar, I've wanted to kiss you." His voice came out as a low growl as he stroked her cheek with his thumb. "I've been crazy about you since the first day we met at the resort, and I haven't been able to stop thinking about you since."

"I haven't been able to stop thinking about you either. Sounds like the whole fated mate thing is what's driving this attraction between us."

"It's actually more than that, you know. I'm not just attracted to you, and I hope you know that."

"I do. And I do because this isn't just a lust thing with me, either. I really like you, Colton, and I think we have a strong connection with each other."

"Can I kiss you, Harper?"

Harper smiled.

"Yes."

He crashed his lips onto hers for a moment before picking her up into his arms.

"Where's your bedroom, Harper?"

"That way. Last door on the left." She said while pointing to a hallway off of the kitchen.

Colton led her into the bedroom and placed her on the bed before removing all of her clothing, as well as his own. He straddled over the length of her body, his dick twitching for her touch as it hovered a mere inch from her sweet, wet center.

"You are so beautiful, Harper." He said as he stroked her hair and kissed her forehead.

She cupped his backside and arched her hips, desperate for his cock to plunge within her.

"I need you, Colton. Now and always."

Colton let out a low growl.

"God, you feel so good wrapped up in my arms."

She dug her nails into his back as his hips rocked against hers. It wasn't long before she began writhing beneath him and became completely undone.

"If you keep doing that, baby, I'll be compelled to give you a love nip." He told her. "We've got tonight and every night after that. No need to rush the love I have for you." He brushed her forehead with a feather-light kiss.

"Somehow, forever doesn't seem long enough with you."

Colton smiled and stroked her hair.

"It's a start, my love. It's a start."

THE END

BEFORE YOU GO...

Enjoyed the book? You can sign up for my newsletter where I offer more fun!

I promise I won't bombard you with tons of emails! I generally write them once a week or once a quarter depending on my writing schedule!

https://www.authoramandakimberley.com/newsletter-signup

ABOUT THE AUTHOR

Amanda Kimberley is a Connecticut native that now lives in the warmth of Northern Texas with her zoo consisting of her husky dog, her tuxedo cat, mice, rabbits, a tank of fish, two daughters, and a husband.

Her nonfiction blog, which focuses on the chronic disease fibromyalgia, has garnered recognition from various organizations, including Health Magazine. Naming her blog, Fibro and Fabulous, as a top blog for fibro sufferers.

When Kimberley is not writing nonfiction, she enjoys penning romance. Her first Furry United Coalition story, The Turtle and the Hare garnered her the 2020 Summer Splash Book Awards of Ink and Scratches for Best Romance.

When she is not writing you can find her cooking whole foods for her pack. She also enjoys reading, hiking, and gaming.

facebook.com/authoramandakimberley

twitter.com/KimberleyLB

instagram.com/amandakimberleylb

bookbub.com/profile/amanda-kimberley

tiktok.com/@amandakimberleylb

ALSO BY AMANDA KIMBERLEY

PNR Series

The Forever Series

Forever Friends

Forever Tied

Forever Cherished

Forever Bound

Forever Immortal

Forever Blood

(Coming Soon)

Forever Loved

(Coming Soon)

Forever Yours

(Coming Soon)

Forever Mine

(Coming Soon)

Historical PNR Series

The Witch Journals Series

Salem's Trial by Judge

Salem's Trial by Township

Salem's Trial by Birth

(Coming Soon)

The Gypsy Witch Trials

(Coming Soon)

Colonial Witch Trials

(Coming Soon)

Stand Alone PNR

The Cure

Manifestations

Uncharted

The Pride Within

Co-Author Stand-Alone PNR

By the Pool with Alex Kimberley

Scifi Fantasy PNR

Suburban Shifter & Celestials Series

Loving the Alpha

Loving the Lone Wolf

Loving the Loup-garou

Loving the Rogue

Loving the Lykos

(Coming Soon)

The Equipoise Solar System Series

Laying Claim to the Lion

Laying Claim to the Legacy

Laying Claim to the Original

(Coming Soon)

Laying Claim to the Dragon

(Coming Soon)

Laying Claim to the Leopard

(Coming Soon)

Laying Claim to the Panda

(Coming Soon)

Laying Claim to the Queen

(Coming Soon)

The Pandemic Series

Pandemic Passion

Pandemic Pandemonium

(Coming Soon)

The Midnight Series

Midnight & Mistletoe

(Coming Soon)

Midnight & Masquerades

(Coming Soon)

Midnight & Magic

(Coming Soon)

Midnight & Memories

(Coming Soon)

Midnight & Mergers

(Coming Soon)

RomCom PNR

The Eve L. Worlds Hellenic Island Shifter Series

The Turtle and the Hare

The Turtle and the Rock

The Ferret and the Fossa

The Leopard and the Llama

(Coming Soon)

Contemporary Romance

The Chronic Collection

Down by the Willow Tree

To Hell With Carpets

Welcome Home

The Chronic Collection

The Just Series

Just Breathe

Just Believe

(Coming Soon)

Just Be

(Coming Soon)

Nonfiction Self Help

The Fibro and Fabulous Series

Fibro and Fabulous: The Book

Fibromyalgia and Sex Can Be a Pain in the Neck

Fibromyalgia and Pregnancy

Poetry

Blue Water Baptism

The Puzzle Called Life

For More Information Please Visit: https://www.bookbub.com/profile/amanda-kimberley

DID YOU LOVE LOVING THE LYKOS? THEN YOU MIGHT LIKE THE PRIDE WITHIN

THE *Pride* WITHIN

USA TODAY BEST SELLING AUTHOR

AMANDA KIMBERLEY

EXCERPT FROM THE PRIDE WITHIN

CHAPTER ONE

"Damn it!" Levi shouted for what seemed like the hundredth time in the past few minutes. "All I'm asking, Google, is for a search that comes up with my uncle in it. Is it really that hard for you?"

He pounded his fingers against the keys in protest to his Ancestry search. All the while he wondered if the hard taps would break the keys. That wouldn't be a good thing since his keyboard was attached to his computer laptop.

"God! This is pointless!" He screamed as he closed the computer. "And what is it going to accomplish anyway? It's not like my parents ever talked about Uncle John. They never talked about any of the family!"

He picked up the letter his cousin sent him and

pulled out the obit. As he traced the photo of his uncle with his index finger, he hoped to get a tangible connection. It was hard to believe his own image stared back at him from the paper. An uncle that looked THAT much like him should have been more prominent in his life. But being his parents broke off ties to the family, it became impossible for him to connect with his great uncle. Anyone with Reis blood seemed a perfect stranger now that he'd become an adult.

The problem wasn't so much his parents as he got older, and he knew that. The blame fell on himself once he got into his twenties. He didn't try to find a way to reach out, and that fell squarely on his shoulders. His grandparents would have been the best bet for getting reconnected. They always hosted early family Sunday brunches that lingered throughout the day. And those visits would have gone into the evenings if his extended family didn't have to take a 2-4 hour drive back home.

None of them lived too far away from Levi while growing up. His grandparents and parents lived in a rural part of Connecticut. Not too far from any major cities like New York, Boston, New Jersey, and Philadelphia. The places where all his relatives lived. He always had legitimate reasons for not visiting his grandparents. And he felt guilty that he didn't have the time to come visit them and the rest of the relatives as he got older.

Life seemed to get in the way when it came to studying for college exams. And working 2-4 jobs to go to college made things difficult. His friends vying for what was left of his time made things worse. In college, the friends won out and he'd find himself hanging out with them until the sun came up on most weekends.

A thought of his best bud Judd Nelson hit his mind, and a smile washed his face. The dude always needed a wingman for the ladies. Levi obliged the request since he got his pick when hanging out with Nelson at the local dives.

Judd's skills at scoping out the ladies when they'd hang out to shoot some pool and darts proved legendary. Levi liked the women Judd picked. These consistently cute women never looked for any long-term attachments. This suited Levi fine because he didn't wish to look for anything permanent either.

He brushed over the obit picture again and read the paragraph they had on his uncle. He seemed to be a loner like Levi because the paragraph made no mention of a wife or kids. Levi frowned a little as he wondered if he'd wind up sharing the same fate as his uncle. At the age of 27, he still had no desire to tie the knot.

Who am I kidding?

He opened up his laptop again and logged into his Facebook account. He went into the photo tab and scrolled until he found Tara Winston's picture. A half-smile formed on his face as he remembered the two glorious weeks they dated two years ago.

She wasn't any prettier than the other girls he had dated, but special in her own right. She was like the girl next door, a girl you'd take to meet your mother, and he wished he didn't let her go. But at the time he was only interested in thinking with the head between his legs. And he knew that that girl deserved more so he broke it off quick.

Even though he would have loved to see how things went, he had no plan of marrying her. He had no intention of marrying any of the girls he dated. He only wanted to have some fun and not be so lonely.

His apartment was about as empty as a bachelor's place would be. There weren't any paintings or pictures on the walls. No tchotchkes on his coffee table. No plants or even a pet. He only had functionally comfortable furniture in his living area and a flat screen. He didn't need anything else.

The kitchen was just as sparse. He wasn't much of a cook unless heating frozen dinners were some kind of culinary art. He only owned a set of four flat dishes, drinking glasses. And none of them matched. Matching stuff was something a girl does for dinner parties. Dinner parties weren't his thing. Judd was the only one who'd come over. They drank from beer bottles, so fancy frosted mugs weren't a priority.

Levi shut the laptop once more and headed for his bedroom. He kicked off his dress shoes and flicked them into the open closet. A large space that only contained two other pairs of footwear, a pair of sneakers and a pair of cowboy boots. He then slid off his tee shirt and jeans and shoved them in a crumpled pile next to his shoes and hopped into his bed. It was just as plain as the rest of his place. He only had it on a simple bed frame with no headboard. His bedding was all black from the sheets to the comforter. The only other piece of furniture in the room was another flat screen.

He flicked on the TV and scrolled through the channels until he settled on the movie John Wick. When Keanu Reeves discovered his dog had died, Levi was already asleep.

EXCERPT FROM THE PRIDE WITHIN
CHAPTER TWO

Layla's alarm blared against the quiet night. She rolled over to shut it off and placed the pillow over her head.

"Why did I agree to take on this stupid case?"

She yelled into the pillow and let out a large sigh before kicking some covers off.

"It should be against the law to have to wake up at 3:30 in the morning to drive to San Antonio from Dallas. UGH! Why did I have to be so stupid? Oh yeah, that's right! I want to make partner." Layla slid out of bed and shuffled into her kitchen to make some coffee. She couldn't deny she needed caffeine before she got into the shower. One cup of the sweet nectar of the gods would not cut it this morning, either. Not with a four and a half-hour drive ahead of her.

Normally her firm would have passed this estate case onto a lawyer living in San Antonio or Houston. But John Reis had been a long-time client and friend to the firm she worked for. Her boss would have seen to the case himself if he didn't have court this morning for another case. Layla got the luck of the draw being the new kid at the firm, still.

She shoved a Death Cups pod into her Keurig and placed a cup underneath. Before closing the lid, she hit the start button. Full pot brewers were now a thing of the past. So when her 12 cups stainless steel and smudge-free brewer bit the big one, she settled on this model in black. It makes small cups to travel-size mugs. The only drawback on days like this had been she needed a full pot to get through the day. For that—she alone missed her 12-cup brewer.

I'm not going to bother with cream and sugar for this one.

She said to herself as she sucked it down in record time. When she had the time to enjoy a cup, she made it light and sweet. When she had to be somewhere and needed to be on top of her game, the darker the coffee, the better. Death Wish Coffee was the darkest and strongest they came. And she was grateful it lacked the awful bitter taste that made her feel thirsty afterward.

After she rinsed out her cup and placed it on the dish rack to dry, she padded into her bedroom again. After picking out a dark pin-stripe pantsuit and black classic pumps, she placed them on her bed. She opened the top drawer of her antique dresser and grabbed miss-matched unmentionables. She placed them with the suit before she hopped into the shower.

Once she toweled herself off, she got dressed, made her bed, and put on some makeup. All before she made another Death Cup for her travel mug. With her briefcase in hand, she dashed out the door. She turned on her car and let it rev for a minute. Then she peered into the briefcase to check that the inheritance papers for Mr. Levi Reis were there. John Reis was Levi's great uncle who owned a large estate in South Africa. He had no children or wife and left everything to his great-nephew, Levi. He spoke often of Levi the few times she had met John Reis in the office.

The man almost tried to set her up with Levi because, as Mr. Reis stated, Levi was only a year older than her. He'd then carry on about how they'd make a cute couple. She always smiled and was polite with Mr. Reis, but she had no intention to meet Levi, even if it was for business. As far as she was concerned, any 27-year-old who wasn't serious with someone yet would never settle. There could be a logical explanation of why he wasn't dating someone seriously at this stage in his life. But usually, any guy who had his family trying to set him up was a player that his family thought a good girl could tame. At least— that's what her Aunt Aviva had always told her anyway.

She wasn't interested in domesticating a man. She could barely take care of herself so she didn't need to have someone in her life that was looking for a mother. She wanted companionship, yes. But she didn't need a burden.

Layla made it in record time to San Antonio. The time on her clock radio read a few minutes before 10AM. She pulled down her visor and peered in the mirror to make sure she looked decent. But she frowned when she saw that her face was shining. She never sweats much in Northern Texas, but the Southern side made her glisten a little too much. She took out her compact and tried to press a little powder under her eyes. It was a feeble attempt to tame her eyeliner so it didn't make her look like a raccoon.

She got out of her car, which she had parked on the street and walked up the driveway. The house was a traditional home with red brick and had accents of terra cotta shutters. The door was a colonial blue and was framed with towering Italian Cypress trees on each side of the door.

She gave the door a light tap. Within a minute a man with tousled chestnut hair and amber-colored eyes answered the door. Layla gaped at the uncanny resemblance the man had with his great uncle. The only difference was that he was the younger version.

"My goodness, you look so much like your uncle!" She found herself saying as she pressed her hand into her chest. Her heart raced. Her palms were all the sudden sweaty. And she needed to find a way to conceal her bubbling nerves in her stomach. The man dripped of sexiness as he slumped over the doorframe in front of her. His bloodshot eyes told her he had just woken up. He clearly was a god when he got out of bed. Not one thing looked out of place and that's so not the hot mess that she was at 3:30 this morning. Hell, she was a hot mess right now, and she had to own it.

The man raked his hair and blinked twice before speaking.

"I'm sorry, you've met my uncle? And you are?"

"Oh, where are my manners! I'm Layla Gallo of Goldstein and Berliner. We represented your late Uncle John Reis. We want to extend our condolences and—"

"Well, thanks for stopping by Layla, but I'm late for work." He said as he raked his chestnut hair once more. It glistened blond highlights when the sun caught it.

"I'm sorry that you are late, but my boss Adam Goldstein told me that he called you and that you're expecting me."

Levi squinted his eyes a bit and pulled out his cell phone. He was trying to remember the night before but was having a difficult time. He had only had one beer, but he seemed to be as fuzzy as if he had had 12. His fitful sleep did him no favors with this woman before him. He clicked on his recent calls and looked at one that came in the night before. His phone said he already saw the message. He squinted again in hopes that the shift in his eyes would make him remember more. But all that he could place was the internet search he did on his distant uncle. He placed his phone back in his pocket. And then the memory finally hit him.

"I didn't think this call was meant for me. I barely knew my Great Uncle John."

Layla narrowed her brows.

"Well, he always spoke fondly of you at our offices. I can assure you this is no mistake, Mr. Levi Reis. I'm here so we can go over the last will and testament of your uncle."

"Last will and testament? Now you've got to be mistaken. Why would I have to look at a last will and testament of someone I didn't know that well? I mean I am related to him, but we were by no means that close."

"Well, the family you claim to not be close to left you his entire estate. Again, I'm sorry that you are late for work, but you are going to have to make other arrangements with your boss. I drove here from the Dallas area early this morning. I need to go over all of this with you and I have no intention of driving back without signatures from you."

"Damn! Really? You've got to be kidding!"

Layla's eyes widened.

"No, Mr. Levi Reis, I'm not kidding you. We need to go over this paperwork and it needs to be today or at the very latest tomorrow. Some of this is time-sensitive." She said with a glare directed straight at him. Layla wasn't a prude by any means. But she certainly wasn't going to have a man she never met swear at her this early in the morning.

Levi blinked again.

"I'm sorry. It's just that you caught me by surprise. Why don't you come in and I'll tell my project manager that I'm taking a day."

Now it was Layla doing the blinking.

"Are you sure he will be fine without you there? I mean, I guess I can wait until tomorrow and drive back here."

"No, you came a long way and I don't like to keep a lady waiting. My manners are better than that—well when I'm more awake they are. Besides —I own the construction company and my manager owes me a day." He said with a wink.

Levi stepped out from the doorframe to allow Layla into his place.

"Would you like some coffee?"

"That would be great."

"Follow me into the kitchen. We can go over this paperwork on the bar top."

Levi grabbed some coffee mugs from one of the cabinets. He then got some pods from the drawer underneath his coffee maker.

"Do you want your coffee strong?"

"Yes, please."

"Cream and sugar?"

"Yes."

Levi reached for the sugar bowl and two spoons. He placed them next to Layla as she was getting out the deed to the house his uncle had owned. His eyes rested on the address that was on the paperwork.

Stratford Castle, South Africa

"This place is in South Africa?"

"Yes. And when you have time, we will take you there so you can see the place. My boss has the keys at the office."

Levi raked his fingers through his thick locks.

"I didn't expect the place to be so far away—let alone another country."

"I can appreciate that. But let's get started so this way you can take the time you need to go out there."

Layla pointed to each line that Levi had to sign. With each line that she was pointing to, Levi's head started to spin faster and faster. He had no idea exactly how much his uncle's net worth was. But he gathered that what he made in a couple of years was probably what his uncle was making in a week. The investments and the house were daunting.

House— no it was a castle. A freaking castle! It even had its own street named after it and it overlooked a golf course.

"Okay there's just one more place that you have to sign, and I'll be out of your hair for the day."

Levi blinked and then focused on Layla's verdant eyes. They looked so lush against her blonde hair and her porcelain skin. His stomach went south as he realized that she would be leaving, and he didn't want her to.

"Why don't we get some lunch after this? You must be hungry and it's an awfully long drive back."

"Oh, I don't want to impose. Besides, there are plenty of drive-thru places while I'm on the road."

"Nonsense! I insist! Besides, I have to do something nice to make up for my crankiness this morning. Do you like Italian? There's this great family-owned place not too far from here called Aldo's. I actually helped them with the construction. We converted an old farmhouse into a restaurant. Well, my dad and I did. I was just a kid when I was helping with the conversion. It's a really nice place and I can get private lunch reservations anytime I want. What do you say?"

Layla's stomach gurgled. She clutched her stomach and giggled.

"I guess my stomach is doing the talking for me. Sure, it sounds good. I haven't had a good Italian meal in what seems like forever."

"Oh?"

"Yeah, my family is originally from upstate New York. I moved here after college when I got a job with Goldstein and Berliner. I love Texas—don't get me wrong—but I miss real Italian food and a good Jewish rye." Layla said as she shrugged. "It's only the little things I miss though. My family's kinda long gone by this point." Layla said as her voice trailed off.

"My family is distant as I'm sure you have gathered by this point, Layla."

"Yeah, I gathered, but at least you still have a family that's among the living. My parents died in a car crash right before my college graduation. They were both only children in their families."

"Oh, now I feel even worse with how I acted towards you earlier."

"Forget about it," Layla said with a dramatically thick New York accent and a wave of her hand. She let out a hearty chuckle before continuing. "Seriously, though, the crash happened a long time ago. I mean I miss them and all of that good food, but I've been handling it for a long while now. Life moves on, you know?"

"Well, I'm not sure if this restaurant will live up to your big city expectations. But I can say it's definitely better than Olive Garden."

Layla laughed again.

"I'm going to hold you to that!"